I0565906

DEAR CRABIGAIL

Criticism, Witticism, and Crime

A sequel to *Bearing Crosses* and *Microwave Is Dead*

By Penny Gardin Lewis

With Contributions by Pam Gardin Gossett and Betty Riden Gardin

Vabella Publishing
P.O. Box 1052
Carrollton, Georgia 30112
www.vabella.com

©Copyright 2021 by Penny Lewis

All rights reserved. No part of the book may be reproduced or utilized in any form or by any means without permission in writing from the author. All requests should be addressed to the publisher.

Cover Illustration and Web Design by Lisa Matheson, Black Squirrel Art Company

Editing by Heather Miller and Dr. Eleanor Hoomes

While some family stories are based on the author's memoirs, this is a work of fiction. Names, characters, businesses, places, events and incidents are either the product of the author's imagination or used in a fictitious manner. Any resemblance to actual persons, living or dead, or actual events is purely coincidental or has been told with the person's permission.

Visit www.dearcrabigail.com and www.pennylewis.press

13-digit ISBN 978-1-942766-80-3

Library of Congress Control Number 2021939575

10 9 8 7 6 5 4 3 2 1

To all the suffering Mothers, but especially mine

Special Thanks

To my Mom, Betty Riden Gardin who tirelessly puts up with my stories about her. She knows that I will exaggerate her quirky, wonderful personality, but she's my biggest fan. I owe my love of writing to her.

To my Twin Sister, Pam who wrote many of the Dear Crabigail answers. She is truly the funniest human being on the planet. I had so much fun including her on this project. Late nights texting Crabigail letters back and forth was a blast. I do owe her an apology for eating garlic toast while she was eating cereal. I really did spoil her breakfast, and for that, I'm kind of sorry. Her "intuitions" and twin-tuning are real.

To my Husband and Muse, Dan I love you. Our conversations often end up in print, and I appreciate your tolerance. 38 years of laughter and love is too great not to share.

To my Listening Friends, Melonie Hopkins and Louise Gentry, thank you for letting me read aloud as I write and edit. Your contributions to the story are more important than you can imagine.

To my Georgia Pen Pal Writing Group: Eleanor, Claire, Cecelia, Beverly, and Donna your gasps and laughter kept me on track. I miss you all.

To my Creative and Hilarious Friend, Lisa Matheson, for your wickedly funny cover design. You captured just what I wanted, to the horror of many.

To my Line Editor, Friend, and Soon-To-Be Published Author of <u>Tho I Be Mute,</u> Heather Miller, you have provided this comma-quotation-dash imperiled writer to look like she has some grammatical sense.

To my Big Picture Editor, Eleanor Hoomes, your support and suggestions have made this a much better story.

To John Bell at Vabella Publishing, I thank you for your tireless efforts to publish books for writers like me.

To my Readers, for buying my books, reading them, sharing them, while laughing, and gasping, and asking for more. Message me on Facebook at Penny Gardin Lewis or email me at pennylewis.press

PROLOGUE

She kissed his forehead. April loved the way her man looked when he slept . . . so at peace. Like her, Adam was a neurosurgeon, and they both spent long hours in the operating room. April needed sleep, too, but the babies in her womb had begun moving. She savored the feeling and rubbed her stomach gently. The double butterfly fluttering made her smile.

They met at a coffee shop in Atlanta across from the hospital on her first day of residency, laughing at the identical orders: Columbian, no sugar, with whipped cream, and a sprinkle of cinnamon. Adam said, "I guess we're twins. Care to share a table?" And she had, drawn by his deep blue eyes and wispy blond hair. Likewise, he was captivated by her charming smile, her short dark curls . . . so dark they were nearly black and piercing brown eyes with flecks of gold. April was tall, nearly as tall as him with a svelte figure and perky breasts. Not too big, not too small. Adam was in love instantly. More so when he learned over that cup of coffee that they shared the same profession. He would supervise her residency, and he was thrilled. Adam liked his women smart.

Physical attraction was important, but they both enjoyed long discussions about politics, the environment, and art. They graduated at the top of their classes and were respected in their matching professions, but they rarely talked about work. It was a relief to discover and share other interests away from the stresses of the hospital. Laughter and love populated every topic, and their passion was feverish and prolific even after long days and nights in the operating room.

April couldn't resist kissing the same spot again on Adam's forehead. He murmured something. She couldn't tell what it was. He didn't seem disturbed. She looked at the clock. It was nearly

1

ninety minutes since he'd fallen asleep and soon he would enter the REM stage. His eyelid flutters would match those in her womb. April leaned closer to confirm.

She reached under her pillow and pulled out a large five-inch nail tied to a string. Her grandmother taught her this trick many years ago. To determine the sex of a child, you twirl the suspended nail and wait for it to settle into a rhythm. And when it did, you looked at which way it swung. If it moved back and forth, the baby, or in this case, babies, would be boys. If the pendulum moved around in circles then the babies would be girls. April didn't know what it would do if she were pregnant with one of each. Adam would scoff at this old wives' tale if he knew, and tell her to wait for a Sonogram. She was a neurosurgeon for God's sake! April didn't care. She held the nail above his forehead, right over the spot where she had kissed him twice.

The nail, really more of a spike than a nail, twirled for a couple of minutes until it began to find its rhythm. When the nail showed her what it wanted to reveal, April smiled. She rested the tip of the nail on Adam's brow, on the sweet kissed spot. And then, retrieving a hammer she had hidden under her pillow, she drove the nail deep into his head.

CR•ℰϽ

CHAPTER 1
AFTER GLOW

The rookie officer hung his blond head about an inch from his foamless, lukewarm mug of beer. He sat next to his dad who drove his cab over from Woodstock to meet up with his boy after he had called him in tears. The father had a sensitive heart, and would never berate his son for crying. Still, he was a little taken aback by it. The boy always seemed so tough, tougher than him anyway.

The father, known to his friends as Albie, to his customers, Mr. Jessup, and to his wife as Albert, slugged away as a typewriter ribbon salesman his whole career. He'd had the whole Southeast as his region, and put twenty thousand miles a year on, first his Buick, then his Caprice. Then, computers came along, of course. He'd told Nadine not to worry as it was just a fad, but he'd been wrong. Not much need for typewriter ribbons anymore, and folks that needed 'em could just order them right from their computers. He had to take an early retirement and was thankful they'd only had one child to support.

That child, Ryan Albert Jessup, had done his self well in school all the way up to the twelfth grade. Albie beamed just thinking about it. His son played football at Woodstock High and then at Georgia State, something Albie always wanted to do himself, but couldn't. The boy had the body for it. Ryan had been a second string quarterback, and Nadine and Albie loved cheering him on from the stands. Albie especially liked that Ryan's blond, good looks and smarts attracted the girls . . . lots of girls. Albie was short and squat, and had been all his life, but not his boy. His boy was big and strong and gifted. Nadine matched Albie in both body and spirit. Her hips were a bit wider than Albie's, and she had to do the fat girl rock . . . back and forth . . . to get enough momentum to get herself up from her chair. She and Albie made quite a pair . . . his and her Humpty

Dumptys. How they'd produced a big, good-lookin' boy like Ryan was still a mystery.

Ryan's marks in a Criminal Justice degree and football heroism had been good, so good, he'd been snapped up by the Police Academy, and he and Nadine stood proudly when he got his shield. After that, Albie, tired of sitting around and inspired by his own son, got out of his recliner and started driving a cab around Woodstock. Nadine didn't mind. She could watch whatever she wanted on the telly, and she always had her knitting. They loved their only son dearly. Now, Nadine was home waiting, and Albie was at some God awful bar with Ryan, and Ryan was crying.

Albie patted Ryan on the back. "Wanta talk about it, Son?"

Ryan shook his head, but started mumbling anyway. "It was the awfullest thing I'd ever seen, Dad. Smelled it first. It was the end of my shift, and I could've, should've let it pass on to the next shift when I got the call, but I didn't."

Albie nodded. He understood dedication. He'd once driven through the worst ice storm Atlanta ever knew to close a deal with the Ted Turner people, only to find out that those folks had the good sense to go home. That's when the Buick became the Caprice thanks to a bad patch of ice on Peachtree.

"Go on, Son."

"This temp partner they put me with, Lonnie, made me go up and check out a report we'd gotten. He stayed in the car. Made me go by myself. He played me, I guess, just so he could laugh about it later . . . you know, Rookie initiation stuff. I had to walk up three flights, 'cause the elevator wouldn't do nothing. I hate those old elevators." Ryan sipped his beer. "The smell got worse and worse at each landing. I pulled my t-shirt up through my shirt collar to cover my mouth and nose. Lotta good that did."

"So, did somebody that lived in that apartment building report the smell?"

"You'd think! It was like that for days. Had to been. But no, it was the building super making rounds that put the call in. He met me at the door of the apartment with the keys. He must've had experience with dead bodies, because he didn't seem bothered at all. I could see out the window on the landing. Lonnie was standing by the car talking on his phone and laughing."

Ryan swirled the last dregs of his beer. His father did the same and signaled the bartender for another round. Two would have to do as he'd have to drive back to Woodstock tonight, and Nadine would have a fit if she smelled alcohol on him. He patted his front pocket to make sure he had a pack of Certs. He felt them and was relieved.

"So you went in and . . . ?"

"I didn't see anything at first. It was dark. I never smelled anything like that before. It was awful. Worse than dead animals on the highway. You've smelled road-killed dogs before, right?" Ryan didn't wait for his father to answer. "The Super flipped on the lights, and they were right there on the sofa. Two girls. They looked just alike. I mean their bodies looked just alike. I guess they were twins."

"Both of them was dead?"

"Yeah. They were naked and their heads had been cut off and their faces were pushed down in their girl parts. Blood was all in the sofa and on the rug."

"Good God, Son."

"Coroner came. He said he didn't know if the heads belonged to the twats they was kissing." Ryan laughed a little at that, but it was a sour laugh. "He made me sick. He was rude and crude. They had names . . . the two girls . . . Cindy and Carol . . . but I didn't know which was which, because they looked just alike in their pictures.

"You couldn't tell if the murderer had switched heads?"

Ryan nodded. "The tops of their necks were crawling with maggots. Coroner said the flies had come and gone. They'd been dead some days. I couldn't help myself. I threw up right there on the ottoman. The boys'll be ribbing me some about that, I reckon. Don't know if Lonnie knows I did that. Probably does."

"Maybe not. They know who done it?"

"No. Too soon. They've already brought Homicide in to investigate, but they made me ride along to tell the parents . . . said I needed the experience."

He started crying again. Albie looked around a bit embarrassed, but nobody seemed to be noticing. He gave Ryan an awkward hug.

"There, there son. It'll be okay."

"I don't think I want to be a police officer no more."

"Now, don't say that. This was your first murder. It'll get better."

Ryan looked sideways at him. Snot filled up both nostrils and oozed in and out as he breathed.

"I hope not, Dad. I hope this kind of stuff never feels better."

CR•SO

Dear Crabigail,

I have good reason to believe that my neighbor across the street has stolen my rocking chair right off of my front porch. I spend many hours there each day, watching and feeding birds. Should I confront her or call the police?

Sincerely,
Lost My Rocker in Cincinnati

Dear Off Yer Rocker,

Sounds to me like yer good neighbor has gone and done you a favor. If you are spending all day sitting on that porch like you say, then you ain't getting any exercise, and you are packing on the pounds. If that's the case, then by now, yer thighs are probably squeezing out the sides of that rocker and embarrassing the whole neighborhood. So get yerself up, and do some jumping jacks and sit squats. If you can't do that, then I suggest buying a porch swing so them thighs of yers has more room to spread out.

Yers,
Crabigail

CR•ED

CHAPTER 2
MOM! IT'S WAY TOO EARLY TO CALL!

I woke to the sound of a ringing phone and a knife blade in the back of my neck . . . sharp and piercing. The pain brought me stingingly awake.

"Get off me!" I screamed. My cat sheathed her claw from my skin and bounded off the bed in pursuit of another victim, most likely the back of the sofa. "It's not too late to have you declawed!" I fumbled for my still ringing phone and looked with one open eye at the clock . . . 6:15. Even for Mom, it was early. She usually waited until at least 6:30 before she called me.

"Morning, Mom." I massaged the wound in the back of my neck. I was still almost face down in my pillow as I talked to my mother.

"Get up! I need you to go to Rome and get your sister.

"What? Why?" I was sure Roxie had drawn blood this time. I turned slightly to see if any was on my finger, but my eyes hadn't adjusted to the morning yet.

"What do you mean, why? Haven't you been watching the news? There is a serial killer in Atlanta, and he is targeting twins."

Nothing excites my mother more than the Atlanta Braves or a good murder. Sometimes, when we played the Dodgers, it was the same thing.

I yawned. "Mom, I live in Carrollton. Pam lives in Rome and . . ."

"What did you say? Your voice sounds muffled."

I turned my head so my mouth was pillow free. "We live a good ways from Atlanta, Mom."

"Close enough. Go and get her. Take Dan with you."

"Mom, I have to . . ."

"I don't care what you're doing. Your sister is helpless up there. Take your car, so you can put her wheelchair in the back."

I sighed . . . or yawned again . . . maybe a combination of the two.

"Why do you think we're targets? How many have been killed?"

"BECAUSE HE'S AFTER TWINS! Two."

"Two sets of twins?"

"No. Two twins. One set."

"Mom! Are you reading Stephen King? It's one murder. Not a series of murders."

"No . . . I . . . am . . . not. And, smarty, he's right here in Georgia! Get up and turn on CNN, and then go to Rome, and get your sister. That awful column she writes . . . that Dear Crabigail thing . . . She needs protecting."

"I notice you aren't worried about me needing protecting."

"Well, she's in a wheelchair, and defenseless, and you have Dan. Take Dan. GO AND GET HER."

"Okay. Can I have coffee first?"

Thirty minutes later, suffering from caffeine withdrawal, the back of my neck stinging from a deep cat-claw puncture, I drove north on Highway 27 to Rome to get my twin sister. I'd left out the serial killer news when I kissed Dan bye, and just told him that Pam needed some help.

I got to Pam's at eight thirty and had to bang on her window to wake her up. Then, I had to wait while she got herself from her bed to her wheelchair, used the bathroom, and turned on the coffee pot. I could hear all these ministrations through the window. She left me standing out on the porch the whole time, getting more irritated by the minute. Finally, she opened the door and wheeled back so I could come in.

"'Bout time! What in the world are you doing in there?"

"What in the world are YOU doing here this early in the morning?"

"I take it you didn't get a 6:45 a.m. serial killer call from Mom?"

"Um, no."

"So much for your psycho psychicness! You didn't feel a cosmic shift in the universe?"

She tilted her head. "No, and I hate when you make fun of my intuitions. You, better than anyone, know they're real."

I did know it. Pam's "intuitions," as she called them, creeped me out. I filled her in on Mom's news and insistence that I come and get her. Then, I helped her pack and carried her suitcase and computer to the car. Pam's Crabigail column was due, and she'd have to write it at my house while, I guess, I stood guard over her. I couldn't help but wonder who would be standing guard over me. I wasn't seriously worried, though.

CR•RO

Dear Crabigail,

I have a corn on my big toe. It's very painful. Do you have a good remedy?

Signed,
Girl from Kansas

Dear Corny Girl,

A . . . CORN? . . . Really? You think you got problems? I got me a bunion the size of a biscuit on the side of my foot. It hurts like the dickens. I've had to go and cut the side of my shoe out just to give it some extra growing room. When I walk over to poke the ashes in my fireplace, that bunion shoots its own sparks right up my shin, through my knee, and into my hoo hoo. So, next time that corn bothers you, just look right down at that itty bitty thang and say, "At least you ain't a bunion."

Yers,
Crabigail

☙•❧

CHAPTER 3
PICTURE HANGER

Her bed had become a hateful place. Carlson, her husband came into their room to tell her the awful thing about their daughters. His face was a sickening greyish color. The area around his lips was white . . . if she could have seen his lips . . . which she couldn't . . . pinched up like he was. "Angie, I have to tell you something. You have to sit up now. And don't scream when I tell you."

She could hear unfamiliar voices downstairs. Puzzled, she'd sat up, pulling the covers up to her chin. Carlson said, "It's about Carol and Cindy." She couldn't process it all, but she knew that he'd said they were dead. She screamed.

The police had come and gone, then, come and gone some more. Her beautiful girls had been murdered. She wanted badly to hear their voices . . . see their beautiful faces. She should have called them after dinner. She hadn't talked to either of them in days. Better, she should have been there. Why hadn't she been there for them? What kind of mother was she?

Carlson wouldn't tell her how and couldn't tell her why, but she'd overheard some of it. She knew that her girl's heads had been cut off like they were pieces of produce ripe for the plucking. She wondered if they had felt it, if they had known what was happening to them. She wondered too, if one had had to watch as the other died. Probably. It added to the terror of it all . . . the thinking like the murderer one moment, her daughters the next. It was beyond terrible . . . recreating how it happened. She wanted to know. She didn't want to know. It changed by the minute.

The police mostly let her alone, directing their questions to her husband in the kitchen at the glass topped mahogany pedestal table with wrought iron upholstered chairs. They were overly courteous, calling him, "Mr. Armstrong" as they made lists of boyfriends both past and current. A fruit bowl sat in the middle of the table with exactly three apples, three oranges, three bananas and two clumps of grapes hanging over each side. One of the officers picked up an apple and turned it in his hands. He returned it to the bowl when he noticed Carlson staring at him. Carlson reached over and moved the apple turning the stem to the top side. Maybe that didn't really happen. Maybe she just imagined Carlson doing that. He liked order.

The investigator came up the stairs to talk to her when she couldn't go down there. He was very respectful and spoke in a low, gravelly voice. Angela had already forgotten his name and what he asked her. A very young officer was with him. He'd stood quietly off to the side with his head bowed. Angela noticed him. Cindy and Carol would have said he was cute. The investigator asked him, "You got anything, Ryan?" The young officer shook his head. Then they left, both of them apologizing for bothering her as they backed out of the bedroom door.

Now, for some reason, she hated the bedroom, especially the bed. The mattress had always been too firm. She'd tried to tell Carlson when they bought it, but he'd said "Angela! It will be better for our backs." And, of course he was right. Carlson was always right. She hated him, too.

Angela went into the hallway and opened the linen closet. Between the King Bamboo sheets and the summer duvet was a nice blue cashmere blanket. Carol gave it to her for Christmas a couple years back. Or maybe it was Cindy? Even she mixed them up sometimes, and she was their mother! . . . WAS their mother . . . Now she was nothing.

Angela carried the blanket downstairs and curled up on the sofa. She wanted a conversation pit that made a nice U shape with ottomans, but Carlson said that would be embarrassing when they had guests over. He helped her pick out a formal sofa. It was an ecru brocade with wooden clawed legs that showed. The pit would have been so much more comfortable. Angela got up and moved to the chair. She tucked her legs under her, pulled the blanket up to her chin, and closed her eyes.

Somewhere in the house, maybe the kitchen, a TV was turned to the news. She heard a woman talking about Carol and Cindy. Then a man said that the police speculated it might be a serial killer, but they didn't know for sure. They probably had her girls' faces up on the screen.

She noticed the pictures were gone from their frames on the way down the stairs. They'd been hard to hang staggered over the staircase like they were. She had prepared to do the job herself . . . had thought all morning how best to do it . . . had formulated a plan . . . Then, her husband came home for lunch and insisted on helping. Carlson used a level and a laser beam gizmo to mark the spots. He'd fussed at her for not having brass picture hanging hooks instead of just nails, and dug through a coffee can in the garage until he found some. Angela's only job was to line up the saw tooth hangers on the back of the frames and drop them over the hooks. Even then, Carlson felt the need to straighten them. That was only a month ago when her babies were still alive.

"Why did Carlson have to give them those?" She looked at the blank spot below the baby pictures and cap and gown shots. He'd given them the glamour shots from the ball. . . her favorites. Carol posed in a black evening gown with a silver clasp on each shoulder, Cindy a sparkly red number. Their blond hair had been French braided and then turned up into a matching knot. The girls never dressed alike, but sometimes, to please their mother, they would wear their hair and makeup the same. The photographs were taken at the Club ball and given to her as a gift by her daughters for her birthday. She wondered again why, of all the photos, Carlson had chosen those. The pictures on the mantel would have been easier to get to.

The TV clicked off, and a moment later, she saw in her peripheral vision her husband come into the living room. She looked over at him. Light was coming through the windows now.

He'd need to be getting ready for work soon she suspected. She had never hated him more.

Carlson walked over to her chair. "Here, Angela. Swallow this." His voice was unusually soft.

She took the pill, and the glass of water, and swallowed the medicine without asking him what it was. Carlson gently took her by the elbow, and helped her up. He set the glass right on the side table without a coaster to protect the wood from damage. So unlike him. Angela was surprised to see that he had been crying. Carlson never cried. His eyes were red and puffy. Together, holding on to one another, they walked up the stairs to their bed.

CR•ЖO

CHAPTER 4
SOMETHING ABOUT PAM

That sister of mine! . . . My twin . . . the constant thorn in my side . . . We fuss and we fight, and say all kinds of snarky and despicable things to one another. Surprisingly, we love each other greatly. We defend one another against the evils of the world, and despite the arguing, we are never ever really mad. Plus, she's the funniest human being on the planet, has mad psychic abilities, and is quite entertaining when she's not getting me killed.

Pam once dragged me into a sordid criminal case that scared the bejeebers out of me. I prefer minding my own business, writing my books, and creating art on my back screened porch. What I don't like is crawling around in weeds, hiding in closets, and peeking through windows at suspected murderers. My twin has an affinity for those activities.

A couple of years back, Pam met me in Carrollton to go on a short trip to the Atlanta High Museum. Thinking she could use some real culture in her life, I talked her into going and would soon regret it.

I noticed that Pam had a distinct lack of energy that, I'm embarrassed to say, annoyed me to no end. We arrived at the museum, and it took forever to get through the door. Pam walked ridiculously slow, and I had to keep stopping to wait for her to catch up. I was eager to see the touring Ansel Adams exhibit, and I admit I was a bit impatient. Finally inside, I made a few disparaging remarks about how out of shape she was.

"Why did you insist on going if you were just gonna drag around?"

"I'm tired. I didn't sleep well last night. I had jumpy legs that kept me awake. Furthermore, I did not insist on going. You talked me into it. I'm only going because you said we'd eat out afterwards at Rays on the River, and I love that place. Besides, I don't see what the big deal is with photographs. Anyone with a phone can take pictures."

"Oh, for Pete's sake! I should've left you home and brought Dan!"

"He didn't want to come either, and you know it. Just go on. I'll catch up."

Pam could only walk a few feet before she had to take a rest on one of the gallery benches. Thirty minutes in, and she was ready to go home. I insisted that she at least wait until we got to "Moonlight, Hernandez, New Mexico," in my mind, Adam's most impressive photograph. She struggled along until I found it. Pam sat down on a carved wooden bench and waited patiently as I examined the piece, thrilled to see it in person.

"I'll just wait here," she said, and began scrolling through Facebook on her phone. Every couple of minutes, her head would dart up, and she'd look at some stranger who was admiring the artwork, completely unaware that my sister, the psychic was reading their inner thoughts..

"Suit yourself." In my head I was thinking, *I swear I'm gonna make her leave the tip at Rays.* I hoped she heard that in my head, as she could sometimes read me like that, too.

I took my time, partly out of spite. I leaned as close as I could to look at the photograph. The moon in all its glory . . . those long wisps of clouds underneath and over the craggy mountains . . . the odd juxtaposition of the cemetery. I was in complete awe and ignored whatever was going on with my sister.

Finally, I said, "Okay, Let's go." I could have stayed another hour, but the fun was just not happening with Pam not participating. Our walk to the parking deck was a nightmare. Pam's gait went from slow to what could best be described as scissor walking. I was afraid she would fall as her right foot overlapped the left in an odd stumbling, drunken-like attempt to push forward. She gasped, "Penny . . . my legs . . . are . . . so heavy."

By the time we got to my Trailblazer, I was supporting her as best I could. My annoyance turned to worry.

A few weeks later at Floyd, her hometown hospital, the family gathered as they took her to surgery. Mom and our younger brother, Brett and I reflected with Pam's children on her strange health issues the last few years. During all of our recent escapades, my sister seemed to be in perfect health. She never had a headache or stomach discomfort of any kind. While menopause came with aching knees and back, and lots of sweat for me, she seemed invincible, and often remarked that she felt better than she had in years. Pam bragged a lot about being "pain free."

Then one day last summer, she burned her arm . . . burned it badly . . . leaning against a hot car. That should have been a huge warning sign to us all. I was shocked when I saw the second degree, possibly third degree damage that spanned a good eight inches up her forearm from wrist to elbow. How in the world could anyone rest their arm on something that hot and not immediately jump away? I was mystified but, since she didn't seem to be in any pain, and the wound eventually healed, I kind of forgot about it.

After our trip to the High, Pam made an appointment with her doctor. Suspecting possible Muscular Sclerosis, she was given a full neurological exam which revealed absolutely nothing. The symptoms worsened.

By February, Pam was nearly paralyzed from the waist down. Her legs just wouldn't work. Admitted to the hospital, more medical tests finally revealed the cause. She had ruptured spinal discs in her neck which is not that uncommon, but nothing that ever happens to my twin is normal. The doctors determined that the rupture actually happened two years or more before. Where anyone else would have been screaming in pain and gotten prompt medical attention, the rupture blocked her pain and temperature sensors. She had no idea, because she felt great. Over time, the oozing goo in her neck continued to drip into her spinal column allowing scar tissue to form.

Surgery stopped the progression of the injury, but the damage was done. On good days, Pam could walk short distances with a walker or a cane. On bad days, she was in a wheelchair. She had to have regular doctor visits because without pain sensors she could go months with a kidney infection or an abscessed tooth and have no idea. In addition to mobility issues, Pam frequently suffered horrible leg spasms that would cause her to uncontrollably yell out. I made a lot of trips to Rome to see after her, to help her with chores, and to drive her to doctor visits, physical therapy, and to the Shepherd Spinal Center in Atlanta.

In the meantime, the press discovered that my sister's special "intuitions" helped solve two major crimes. They loved to write about her, and would include a mention about the mysterious disappearance of her husband, Sam. Pam's intuitions seemed to have a block where he was concerned. She referred to him all the time as "S. H." which most people thought meant "Sam Hill," but family knew really stood for "Shithead." Pam never seemed to care if he ever came back, and was happy as a clam without him in her life. I doubt she'd focus her intuitive mind in his direction, whatever direction that was, even if she could. He truly was a shithead, so I couldn't blame her.

The press just couldn't get enough of my sister, which was great, because I went out of my way to avoid them, and she could have them. She was totally accessible to reporters, and they seemed to love that she was in a wheelchair . . . probably gave them some ADA points or something. Mostly, they loved her provable and mysterious psychic skills.

All of this attention led to Pam getting a job at the local Rome newspaper, making predictions for folks who wrote in about their personal lives. I thought this was a great job for her and gave her back some focus she lost with her medically-induced retirement as a teacher of the blind. Plus, it distracted her away from dragging me into more murder investigations that I certainly was not cut out for.

Pam loved her job at the paper, which allowed her to work from home. Most people who write these types of columns focus on the positive. Like they will "predict" that a new job is on the horizon, or boat loads of money will fall at the letter writer's feet, or a handsome Prince will whisk them away . . . but not Pam. Pam told the letter writers exactly what she saw.

One poor bride-to-be wrote, "Dear Pam, I'm getting married in June. Will my wedding day be all that I want it to be?" Pam replied, "No. On the morning of your wedding you will find a zit as big as a dime on your chin. Everyone, including the groom, will stare at it all during the ceremony and reception, but the flowers will be real pretty."

Another writer asked, "Will I get promoted this year?" Pam's answer was, "Yes, you will. But, only because you agree to sleep with the boss and totally ruin his marriage and yours."

After a few of those, and many complaints, the newspaper publisher met with Pam and a new plan was formed. It turned out that Mr. Grayson, the publisher, had a sense of humor. He agreed with the complainers that my sister's columns were awful, but he saw potential to go a completely different route. With his guidance, Pam started writing under the pseudonym "Dear Crabigail." The column was deliberately mean, but funny. Crabigail pointedly never actually helped anyone. In the beginning Mr. Grayson wrote all of the questions, and Pam the answers. But, as Pam's popularity grew, fans sent enough questions to the paper the publisher was able to back off. The fans did a great job of setting Pam up with questions that would lead to hilarious responses. Her column was an instant hit and, within a year, it was syndicated in 150 newspapers nationwide. My sister was famous.

At Pam's request, I contributed the Crabigail doppelganger. After months of looking through grouchy old lady pictures, I finally had a brainstorm. I drove to Rome and took pictures of my sister, used software to age progress the best of them, superimposed a cigarette drooping out of her mouth, and Waa La! Crabigail sprouted hideously into the public eye.

Unfortunately, Pam's new fame came with many, many requests to appear on talk shows, conferences and other events. A chance to appear on the Tonight Show, The Today Show, and Dr. Phil would be a thrill for most folks, and the National attention should have been exciting for my sister, but Pam had a terror of flying, and had never been on an airplane despite growing up in an Air Force family. I would have gone with her on all of these and helped her, but no. Despite the possibilities each opportunity provided, she absolutely refused to go.

CR•SO

Dear Crabigail,

Is it okay to have sex before marriage? I am 87 and he is 88.

Sincerely,
Wrinkley in Berkley

Dear Wrinkled Up Old Prune,

You ever hear that sayin, "Why buy the cow if'n you can git the milk fer free?" Well I say, "Why buy the hog fer a little sausage?" Men's wiggly parts git a little soft when they git older so I say, "go ahead with yer old self and try before ya buy, if'n you wanta make sure that sausage ain't shriveled into jerky."

Yers,
Crabigail

CR•ƎƆ

CHAPTER 5
PARTNER

Ryan Jessup completed his neatly typed report on the domestic he'd spent the last few hours handling. He rubbed his stinging neck. The incident was typical and cliché: a drunk boyfriend in a wife beater t-shirt blackened his just-as-drunk girlfriend's eye. The skinny buck-toothed girlfriend fought like an alley cat when Ryan and his training partner of the night, Clarence, tried to arrest the boyfriend. She had leaped on his back and Clarence and the boyfriend had the dickens of a time prying her loose. Ryan had scratch marks on his neck to show for it. The girl would probably spend more time locked up than the boyfriend because she wouldn't think of pressing charges against her love bunny. Six months on the force and Ryan was getting a handle on the futility of much of his job.

He put his paperwork in the tray on the Sarge's desk and turned towards the door, ready to meet his dad for a beer. Their Friday night bar meetings were one of the highlights of Ryan's week. He knew it meant a lot to his dad, too.

"Hold up there, Spud."

He looked back at his Sergeant. "Sir?"

"Somebody in the back office need to jaw witcha."

"Who?"

The Sergeant shrugged, and Ryan could see that he'd been dismissed. Probably Clarence trying to push his own paperwork off on the rookie. No dice.

Ryan walked into the overly lit, olive green painted office and tilted his head in wonder at the large, handsome black man sitting at the desk pouring over a file. He'd never seen this detective before.

"You wanted to see me, Sir?"

Ryan was taken aback when the man stood. He towered over the rookie in a blue suit with a blue and white striped tie and heavily starched white shirt. His shoes were spit shined. If Ryan had to guess, he'd say the man was six-foot-six, two- hundred and eighty muscle-packed pounds. The man was intimidating by stature alone, so it was incongruous when he smiled.

"Hello, son. I know you want to get out of here and meet up with your dad, so I'll make this quick."

Ryan couldn't have been more surprised.

The man held his hand out and firmly grasped Ryan's in the time-honored custom of a good handshake. "Jim Candor. FBI." He let go of Ryan's hand and displayed the ID badge he'd pulled from his shirt pocket.

"Okay?"

"Like I said, I'm going to make this quick. You were one of the officers who found the two girls in the twin murder case.

"Actually, I was by myself. My partner was in the car."

Agent Candor nodded. He already knew that. "Must have been traumatic."

"It was terrible. I won't pretend it wasn't. What do you need to know, Sir?"

"I'm not here for information. I'm here for help. With your police chief's permission, I've requested that you be reassigned to me in a joint investigation requested by your Governor. The Sergeant out front has the paperwork for the transfer."

Ryan was shocked. "Why me? . . . I mean, Sir . . . I don't understand. I mean I'm a rookie, been here six months, not even six months. Why me?"

The FBI Agent held up his hand. "First of all, I've checked you out, and I think we'll work well together. You have a sensitivity that will be beneficial meeting with the parents of the victims. I think they'll like you. Second of all, stop calling me 'Sir.' It's 'Jim.' Call me 'Jim.'"

"Yes, Sir. And thank you Sir." Ryan blushed.

"This won't be a long assignment, I assure you. Probably a day or two. I was in Atlanta working the final details on an old case, when I got this call. It's not the kind of thing the FBI usually handles. Apparently, there's some political pressure here. So, you and I will give it a quick look over. See if we can help. You okay with that?"

Ryan nodded. He was scared, and thrilled, and most certainly intimidated.

Agent Candor clapped Ryan on the back. "C'mon, let's get your paperwork, and you go on and see your dad. He oughta be real proud. I'll meet you here in the morning. I'm temporarily using this room as my office, so you come here.

"Yes, Sir. I will." Ryan hadn't even mentioned meeting his dad.

"Ryan, seriously . . ."

"Jim. Sir." Ryan could feel his cheeks redden even more.

CR•ℬ

CHAPTER 6
HEMP ROPE

The boy, Aaron, just turned seventeen, sported a scruffy wisp of a nothing beard and ridiculous huge, black buttons in his ears. He stood behind the cash register in Herman's Cash and Carry Supply Store. Aaron leafed through a magazine and took a bite of a stolen Snicker's Bar he swiped from the checkout aisle's impulse shelf. There had only been two customers all day, which was just how Aaron liked it. When the bell dingled, Aaron jumped and hid the Snickers behind the rags and Windex on the ledge below the register.

At first, Aaron was relieved that it wasn't his boss and reached for his Snickers, but when he looked into the eyes of the customer, there was something there that made his skin crawl and he reached, instead, for the Windex. The absurdity of the choice of weapon wouldn't hit him until hours later when he lay in his twin bed thinking about the black-pooled soulless eyes that seemed to see into the back of his head.

"Can I help you?"

No answer. The killer, the customer, picked up a carry basket and walked down the aisle looking for whatever killer customers need that day.

The boy watched the killer customer shop, his magazine forgotten. The killer customer found a roll of braided hemp rope, shaking the dust off of it, before dropping the roll into the red carry basket. A box of five-inch carabiners, the largest size Herman's Cash and Carry stocked, and a roll of off brand duct tape were selected next and last.

All of this could have been bought at Home Depot, but the killer customer knew better. Dumb in this day and age to not have security cameras, but that meant no footage of the purchase, while cash made tracing the transaction near impossible.

The killer customer sat the basket on the counter and laid three twenties beside it.

"You going climbing?"

No response . . . not even a shake of the head.

"Tying down some furniture? Must be a lot of dang furniture!"

The no response awkward silence lasted until the boy twisted his lip ring and finally put the items in a bag.

"You come back now."

The bell rang again as the door closed.

"Rude!" The boy went back to his "Car Craft" magazine making sure not to crease the pages, so he could rerack it later. He was soon drooling over the expensive cars and bikes on the glossy pages . . . cars and bikes he would never own, and forgot all about his rude, furniture-strapping, mountain-climbing, killer customer. He finished his Snickers and tore open a bag of Peanut M&Ms. Aaron forgot about the whole incident until he reflected about it that night, shivering in his twin bed, picking at a zit that had popped up just that day, while he stared at the peeling paint of his bedroom ceiling.

CR•ᔥ

Dear Crabigail,

My husband wants to name our baby boy after himself when it's born. It's not that I hate his name. I've just never liked the idea of a Junior, as I think children should have their own identities. How can I tell my husband without hurting his feelings?

Signed,
Mrs. Bulbous Blabner

Dear Ain't You Saddled With An Awful Name?

I say if the name is a good one, then you should get as much use as possible out of it to keep it going. My husband, John Earl, never give me a son. So, I just call ever lizard, snake, and rat that crawls across our lawn, John Earl, too. I'm sure he appreciates the honor.

Yers,
Crabigail

CR•ℰO

CHAPTER 7
LIZZIE'S CANYON

My best friend, Lizzie stopped by the house to see Pam and eat lunch. She told us, between mouthfuls of tuna salad, about her pending camping trip to the Grand Canyon. She was leaving the next day with a group assembled from her weekly trivia game and triggered by a winning question from a few Tuesday nights before.

I cracked up. "Excuse me. YOU are going to sleep in a sleeping bag in the Grand Canyon?"

"Sure am. Why not? We fly there in the morning."

"Lizzie! You are the person who called an exterminator ten times because you saw a fly every time you walked to your mailbox."

Lizzie was born and raised in Florida where bugs are plentiful, but you wouldn't know it the way she complained.

"I don't like bugs. So what? I'll wear bug spray."

"Bug spray won't keep away the rattlesnakes."

"No. No. No. You're wrong. I asked the travel agent about snakes, and she assured me that all snakes had been removed from the Grand Canyon."

"That is utterly ridiculous. Have you ever seen how big the canyons are?"

"Well, no . . . just in pictures . . . but, I believe the agent. Why would she lie?"

"How about to make a sale to a gullible, critter-scared woman?"

Lizzie left around three. Pam watched TV while I painted. Dan would be home sometime before six, and he would be hungry.

I was tired, and tired cooking was pretty much always spaghetti. I took the pasta and jarred sauce out of the cabinet. Pam would fuss that I didn't make it from scratch, but that was just too bad. She didn't say a word though, and she and Dan chatted over garlic bread and pasta. Later that evening, we were watching TV when Lizzie called. I muted the TV and Pam turned on the speaker.

"OH EM GEE," she said. "You were right. I've been Googling the Grand Canyon ever since I got home. Did you know that the most poisonous snake in the United States is CALLED the Grand Canyon Rattlesnake?

I looked at Dan. He was grinning. Pam had told him about Lizzie's big adventure.

"Venomous."

"What? What's that Penny?"

"It's venomous, not poisonous. If you get hungry out there in the wilderness, you can cook up a batch of rattlesnakes and eat them."

"Eww . . . Gross. I don't know how I'm even friends with you. But, it doesn't matter. I'm still going. I found out from Google that there are things I can do to protect myself. Snakes like rocks. So, if I put my sleeping bag out in the open, and away from the rocks, they'll leave me alone.

Pam was listening and piped in. "I hope that works for you, Lizzie."

I had a couch cushion pressed against my mouth so that Lizzie couldn't hear me laughing. Dan was doing that silent chuckle thing that he does sometimes.

A couple of days later, Lizzie called. I hit the speaker button so Pam could hear.

"You are not going to believe what happened to me! Hey, Pam. Are you still at Penny's? Anyway Penny, I'm never coming here again. And if you were my friends you would have stopped me."

Pam was giggling. "What in the world happened, Lizzie?"

"I'll just tell you! I did what I told you I was going to do. I put my sleeping bag WAY out in the open. No one else believed me when I told them why. They put theirs up against the rocks to keep sheltered from the wind. I didn't CARE about the wind. I didn't even care about the cute travel guide sleeping by the rocks. I CARED about snakes. I told them they were fools, but they wouldn't listen."

"Uh oh. Did one of them get snake bit?"

"NO! JUST LISTEN. This morning I woke up. I sat up to stretch and looked to my left at the sleeping bags. Everyone at the rocks was still sleeping." The tone in Lizzie's voice turned ominous. "And then I looked down. Right beside me . . . RIGHT BESIDE ME . . . was an S shaped trail in the sand, about four inches wide, that started from the rocks over where my friends were. The trail stopped right by my left leg. I looked on the right side of my sleeping bag." Her voice got louder with sort of a squealy pitch. "The SAME S shaped trail started AGAIN, RIGHT THERE on the other side of me, and then off in to some rocks."

Pam and I were both laughing hysterically. I grabbed the mouth muffling couch cushion.

Pam asked, "Oh my goodness, Lizzie. A rattlesnake crawled over you in the night?"

"YES! A DAMN RATTLESNAKE CRAWLED ACROSS MY BODY WHILE I WAS SLEEPING!"

"Why are you yelling at us? We didn't put snakes in the Grand Canyon."

Lizzie didn't answer. I'm sure she was annoyed that we were laughing.

I asked, "So are you going to move near the rocks tonight with everyone else?"

Now she was composed and haughty. "No, I most certainly will not!"

"Well, where will you put your sleeping bag?"

"I'll TELL you where I already put it! I put it at the Best Western!"

Pam hung out at my house for a week and then, despite Mom's protestations, she insisted that I take her home, saying, "One set of dead twins does not a serial killer make." I agreed and took her home.

CR•ℬ

CHAPTER 8
SISTER SECRET

We were half way back to Rome when Pam said, "Penny, pull over."

I turned off the road and pulled into a convenience store, parking at the curb near the road.

"What are we stopping for?"

She looked at me sadly. "Okay. So, I have something to tell you in case anything happens to me."

"Oh good grief!" Then I caught my breath. She was finally going to tell me what happened to SH, her husband gone missing for eight years.

"I've left an envelope with directions in the top left drawer of my desk. It has your name on it."

"All right." This is it. She's going to tell me the truth . . . where SH has been all this time . . . where his body is hid. "Directions to what?"

"My jam."

"Excuse me?"

"Step by step directions to make my Pam Jam."

"You can't be serious. Good Lord in Heaven fishing with the angels, I'm not going to make your jam."

"Yes, you will. Christmases will come, and the family will be so sad that they don't get a box full of Pam Jams. You'll feel bad and wish you had the recipes and directions and you'll want real bad to make it. The family will be looking at you in disappointment . . . judging you. You can't let them down.

I sighed. "Okay. But, you have to do something for me, too."

"I really don't, but go ahead and try me."

"If I die first, you have to come to my house every month in the summer and put flea medicine on Roxie. Dan will never remember to do that."

"She'll bite me."

"Jam making will burn me. You know it, and I know it."

"I guess that's fair. I'll do it. If you get killed, I'll come and de-flea your cat." With that assurance, I backed up and pulled onto the highway, heading north towards Rome.

Pam was quiet for a minute. "Of course, if Mom is right, and this is a serial killer murdering twins, we'll probably die together."

I had nothing to add to that. "Want me and Dan to pick you up for Thanksgiving?"

My sister shook her head. "Nah! Jennifer will take me. Just get to Mom's early. It's your turn to peel potatoes."

☙•❧

Dear Crabigail,

Cheesecake or carrot cake or is it reasonable to eat both? I have an obsession with cake and need some advice to lay off the calories.

Thanks,
On the Scales in Wales

Dear Big as a Whale,

Got my canning done, and even though I'm plum tuckered out, I thought I'd hep you. I ain't never keered much for carrot cake. I ain't actually ever tried it, but carrots give me the gas bubbles. I used to take my youngins and the neighbor boys to them churches that was having them covered dish dinners, cause ya know, free food. Anyways, I noticed the boys was gobbling up the carrot cake. So, I thought, well that's one way to git vegetables in em. But I ain't gonna make a cake I can't eat my own self, so I came up with my own recipe.

CRABIGAIL'S BUTTER BEAN CAKE
Ingredients
1 Box of Cake Mix
1 Can of Butterbeans
Whatever the back of the cake box says to put in it

DIRECTIONS
Read the back of the box and do what it says then add the can of butter beans. You can substitute okra or pintos if ya want. Bake it up. If folks are hungry enough they'll eat it.

Yers,
Crabigail

ଔ•ଔ

CHAPTER 9
BINGO PRIZE

Ebodine Washington was sometimes late for church, often really. The widow ladies of the First Christian Apostolic Church of the Redeemer always tsk tsked her as she sailed in at ten after with an embarrassed Stanley following right behind. Ebodine didn't give a flying flip what they thought. Sunday last, not three feet from the door, she'd called it the First Christian "Apathetic" Church of duh Redeemer. After all, the brick sign outside read "We are Satisfied with Jesus."

"What kinda commitment is that?" she'd asked Stanley, her ample breasts thrust in the air in indignation. Ebodine adjusted her red hat with white poppies and wide black band so that she could look her husband square on. Stanley was almost a deacon and served on the property committee and had personally approved the signage. He'd tried to explain to Ebodine that it was from a song.

"Why, Ebodine! Brother Purvis picked that line right from Hymn number . . ."

Ebodine threw up her big mahogany hand which sported finely manicured long red nails and quite the assortment of garishly large gemstone rings. Though she had never struck Stanley and never would, he feared that mighty hand as if he'd turn to a pillar of salt if he didn't. And so, he'd quit trying to explain it to his wife and stopped right there mid-sentence. Ebodine kept that hand up in the air and sailed right on by her husband and up the church steps. Anyone watching from a distance would've thought Ebodine was praising Jesus, but no one was there to see 'cept Stanley. Everyone else had made it on time and was already seated in their pew.

Shorter than Ebodine by a foot and lighter by a hundred pounds, Stanley had a hard time standing up to his wife. He'd wince that she wouldn't find a seat in the back, but would parade in with such pomp that the preacher would stop praying or praising until they'd settled into the third pew from the front. . .The Washington pew as it was called by those who dared not sit there even at five after on an Easter Sunday. It was sometimes said by the widow ladies that it was no wonder the couple's four grown children, Franklin 30, Shanelle 27, and the twins Jolene and Julene . . . just turned 21 . . . called their own mama a bully.

Church wasn't the only thing she was late for. Ebodine never made it on time for checkups with Dr. Geerson and dared the nurses to cancel her appointments. They never did and just bumped her to the front whenever she arrived. Dr. Geerson treated Ebodine like a queen. He'd even let her set herself down in the room's upholstered chair and never required her to climb up on the exam table.

Ebodine was even tardy to the votin' polls, and would slam open the closed door at the Peachtree Community Center yelling, "One more voter here!" The volunteers were used to it and politely escorted Ebodine to the fake polling booth they'd made for her despite the state law that ended voting ten to twenty minutes earlier. Mrs. Clementine would hand her a paper ballot that she crafted herself on her fat monitored old computer at home. Voters hadn't used paper ballots since 1995, but Ebodine didn't know that. Mr. Davies would give her a finely sharpened #2 yellow pencil with an unsullied pink eraser. Ebodine would take her time shading in her votes while the tired poll workers boxed up the rest of the room. She spent more time chewing on her pencil than she did shading. When Ebodine finished voting, she would write her opinions on the state of politics all over the ballot, running up and across every margin. She had a lot to say about both Democrats and Republicans and about issues ranging from education to dog catching. She wasn't averse at throwing in a few four letter curse words that would have horrified the preacher, the Deacons, Stanley, and of course the widow ladies of The First Christian Apostolic Church of the Redeemer. Ebodine would not have cared, but she would have been real sore had she known her vote hadn't counted in years.

"Ebodine, you'll be late to your own funeral," Stanley once muttered. He was always muttering about something.

"Good!" she said. "Who wants ta go ta duh grave early?"

One place Ebodine never arrived late to was Wednesday night Bingo at the Am Vets around the corner and down two blocks from the big church Dr. King used to preach at. As a matter of fact, she arrived early each week.

Ebodine dressed in her black stretch pants and green tunic with a gauzy light-weight jacket that flowed to her knees in a cascade of assorted spring flowers, birds, and butterflies. From her closet, she picked out black flats with red bows and sat on the bed to fit them to her swollen feet. She slid her rings on her fingers, and then wiggled her right hand, trying to decide, in front of the row of Styrofoam heads on her dresser. Each of the seven heads held a coiffured wig, each a different style and color. She chose a red, curly wig with blond tips and positioned it carefully on her head. The final touch was a generous helping of Jean Nate body spray and a swath of cherry red lipstick. She kissed Stanley bye on top of his head leaving a big red lip print on his bald spot. Ebodine told him there was extra potato salad in the fridge if he wanted it and loaf bread if his roll weren't enough. Stanley nodded over his plate. This was a weekly routine.

Ebodine walked out the door to the street and to her car. She started the engine of her 1982 pearl white Chrysler and grumbled as the radio came on.

" . . . *for information leading to the arrest of whoever is responsible for a gruesome murder of twi . . .*"

She turned the knob that silenced her radio. "I ain't got time for that mess." It would have taken Ebodine five minutes or more to find her gospel station. Stanley was always switching up her radio from FM 102.5 WPZE to that AM yackety news show.

Folks going on and on about murders and robberies! She planned to wake him up to fuss about it when she got home.

Ebodine sat in her parking space perusing the road, waiting for traffic to clear completely before making her left turn on to Irwin Avenue. Street side parking was such a nuisance. One day she'd like to have a house with a garage or at least a carport. Heck, a driveway would be a one up. She told Stanley over and over.

She checked the analog clock on the dash. 6:15. Bingo didn't start 'til seven, but early birds like her got the good seats away from the band and near the caller. The band could go as far as she was concerned, but the young people would be there in force to bump and grind in pornographic ways, and Ebodine wanted to sit far on the other side and away from that mess where she could hear and avoid the distraction. Plus, she could get first pick of the Bingo cards. Ebodine couldn't stand getting dog-eared, old ones. She usually bought eight cards at $3 apiece, but bless his heart, Stanley had given her thirty, that night, and so she could get ten. Maybe she'd let him sleep, after all.

"Laws, I hope Minnie's there to hep me keep up with em." Minnie only ever bought one or two Bingo cards and would help Ebodine find her numbers. She bellowed in glee and pounded the dash with the flat of her hand. The prizes that night included some hundred dollar pots and a flat screen TV. "If'n I win a big pot, I'll give Minnie five or ten." She said this out loud, knowing she'd do no such thing.

Ebodine signaled right a few yards from Courtland Street. She began humming and smiling. As she made the turn, she saw the bum who was always on the corner and quickly looked away. She didn't like to make eye contact with panhandlers. As she passed him by, he ran into the road behind her and jumped up and down waving like the maniac he was. Ebodine could see him in the rear view and pursed her lips and sped up a bit . . . not much though. Anything over twenty-five made Ebodine pump the brakes. She passed a nice looking black man in a blue suit and looked back to see him acting just like the bum. The durn fool was in the street pointing and yelling and waving his briefcase over his head. She hadn't done a thing wrong and tootled on down the road. She could see the man with his cell phone to his ear. "Idiot!" she mumbled and then smiled. These crazy men would not spoil her mood.

As she looked in her mirror again, she saw another car make the turn. He drove a little fast for Sweet Auburn if you asked Ebodine her opinion, and he was soon right up behind her. The driver, a silver haired older white man began blowing his horn and waving his arm out the window signaling her to pull over.

"The nerve! What's wrong wit dese men?" Ebodine had no intention of pulling over to let the man pass and continued driving 20 miles an hour. Anything faster than that was just nonsense.

As she reached Decatur Street, the man passed her on the left. He had his window down yelling at her, but Ebodine looked straight ahead and ignored him.

The old man slowed in front of her. She could see he was also on his phone. "They should outlaw dem things."

"Ass!" Ebodine could say, *Ass*. It was in the Holy Bible. "You better not make me late for Bingo."

Blue lights and sirens came from behind. This was one of the reasons Ebodine drove slow. Always sirens of some kind in Atlanta. They'd pass her by.

Only this time they didn't. The way they was pulling up close behind her made her think they was pulling her over. HER!

"Lordamercy! Dem boys gonna make me late some."

Ebodine stopped right in the middle of the road and waited, expecting they'd zoom around her to chase after some robber or murderer. Two more police cars roared through the light in front of her hemming her in on three sides.

"What in the God's green mercy have I done?"

Stanley was always puzzled when she used that particular expression. He, nor anyone else, knew what it meant, but she said it all the time.

Ebodine reached for her purse to find her license when she heard an officer behind her on some kind of loud speaker. He said, "Lady, we need you to step outa your car and keep your hands up."

Ebodine decided she'd do no such thing. All her Bingo friends would be driving by and would see her being treated like a criminal. HER! And Stanley being almost a deacon! They'd have to shoot her first.

Ryan sat in the passenger seat of patrolman Marcus's police cruiser. Ryan hadn't been assigned a real partner yet. As a Rookie, he would mostly fill in for officers on leave. Some temporary partners liked to give him grandfatherly advice. Others resented his young good looks and inexperience and could be downright mean. Marcus fell somewhere in the middle. They had gotten the call about the lady in the white Chrysler and were in the car nearly touching front bumper to front bumper.

Ryan looked over at Marcus. Marcus had his eyebrows knitted together and his lips pressed so tight you couldn't see them. Ryan was nervous, but dutifully he opened his door and got out. "Oh, God!"

"I got this," Marcus said. Marcus had sized up the old lady. She reminded him of his mother in her big brimmed hat and colored wig and he decided quickly that she was no threat. He waved off the rear officer who had drawn his gun along with the partner wielding the bullhorn.

Marcus tapped on Ebodine's window. "Mama, you can just sit there if you want, but me and my partner here are gonna take a look at the back end of your car."

"What in the world!" Ebodine opened the door and let Ryan help her to her feet. She followed the officers to the rear. When she saw what she saw her legs crumbled and Marcus and Ryan had to hold her up.

"Laws, Laws, Laws! Who done that to my car?"

Hemp rope looped across and around Ebodine's bumper, round and round where it ended in the middle with a big knot. Tucked into the rope on the left was a severed human arm and to the right, a leg that had been cut off below the knee. Ryan and Marcus could see there wasn't much blood. The cutting had been done after death.

"Somebody gotta call Stanley for me. STANLEY! I NEED STANLEY!"

Ryan, still holding her up, said, "I'm so sorry Ma'am. You'll need to go to the station with us. We can call your husband . . . I assume that's Stanley . . . from there.

"Dem's black people's body parts. Oh my Lord."

"Yes'm, they are."

"Whose? Who'd do such a thing?"

"We don't know, Ma'am, but we'll find out. Right now we have to get investigators out here and take you down for an interview."

"My car?" Ebodine's voice was weaker.

Ryan didn't know and looked at Marcus.

Marcus shrugged and said, "It'll get towed at some point I reckon. We'll let you know. Now come with us, Mama."

"I have Bingo," . . . Almost a whisper. . .

"Pardon me, Ma'am?" Ryan wasn't sure if he heard right.

"I have Bingo. It's Wednesday night. Will I still be able to go?"

Ryan was surprised. "No, Ma'am. Not this week."

Ebodine nodded and allowed the officers to walk her to their cruiser.

Later that night, they let her call Stanley and she blubbered out the whole story, at least what she knew of it. They only had the one car, and it had been impounded, so Stanley told her that he'd call their son, Franklin, to come and get her. Officers Ryan and Marcus offered to take her home, but she'd had enough of them and the whole nasty situation.

Franklin stopped by his sister's apartment on the way to get his mom and told Shanelle the awful story. Shanelle called the twins, but they didn't answer. Jolene and Julene shared a brownstone not far from their parents. They both worked at Macy's downtown and were usually home in the evening unless they had dates. Shanelle called her dad to check on him and told him to please let the twins know what happened. Bully or not, their mother needed them, and they would come together as a family.

Stanley muttered as he walked to the Brownstone. "Laws! What is this world a coming to?" He knew there'd be no living with Ebodine. She'd milk this trauma for months, including the fact that this mess'd probably make her late for Bingo. Stanley had no way of knowing that Ebodine would never be late for anything again, because, until the day she died some twenty years later, she would never leave their house . . . not for Church . . . . not for the Doctor's . . . not for the voting poll . . . not even for Bingo.

Stanley could see the girls cars parked out front. When they didn't answer, he looked through the front window. Stanley's legs dissolved under him right there on the front porch, screaming a silent plea, clawing up at the window. His girls, his twins, were sitting together on the blood saturated sofa. Jolene was missing an arm, Julene part of a leg. Their eyes looked straight ahead at nothing.

CR•ഌ

CHAPTER 10
UNLIKELY TEAM

Jim and Ryan met across a peeling, metal desk in the makeshift office. Crime scene photos from the Armstrong and Washington twins hung on the army green block wall in a gruesome mosaic. Sticky notes with scribbles from both the officer and the detective were randomly adhered on and around the photos. They sat quietly sipping not so bad black coffee from Styrofoam cups as they poured over matching coroner reports. Empty cups with dried black sludge and cracker wrappers lay off to the side.

Ryan hated to interrupt Jim's concentration, but he had a question. "Do you think you can officially call him a serial killer yet?"

Jim shrugged.

"Do you think he will stick with women? Is it gonna be a pattern?"

Jim looked up. There was a long pause before he spoke. "Probably. D.C. office thinks so. But who knows? I'd like to catch him before we see a pattern. Right now, we got nothing. Everyone's a suspect until they're not."

It was Ryan's turn to nod.

"Jim, what I don't understand is the cutting off body parts. He doesn't take them with him. What's the point?"

"I don't know. I'll say this, though. The precision of the cuts, the Coroner confirms this, they are really precise. Well done. You follow me?"

"You think it might be a doctor or someone in the medical profession?"

"I do. We should be getting a profile from Quantico soon. Ordinarily we don't step in this early, but the Governor of your great state asked us to. He's friends with the first family, the Armstrongs."

"So, there is political pressure?" Ryan asked.

"Not as much as you would think. It was more of a plea for help. I think the authorities here knew from the first case that this had the look of something evil, and that those girls wouldn't be an isolated case. They were right. It's unusual for the FBI to be involved this early and we will pull out all the resources we can. We are going to see more, you know."

"It's horrible what he's doing."

"Ryan, I know it's difficult, but you have to disconnect from this emotionally. It could get real bad here or resolve quickly. Who knows? But, when you go home, listen to music. Talk to your dad. Watch sports or QVC or porn or whatever you're into, but don't dream about this when you go home at night."

Ryan blushed. It was too late for that. His dreams were terrifying. Even Candy couldn't help.

"Ms. Washington . . . Ebodine. I felt so bad for her today. She made those screams . . . those horrible sounds when we met with her. I felt sorry for her husband, too. He just looked so helpless. I thought of my own parents. Broke my heart."

"I know. The Armstrongs were the same way. Good families, both of them."

"You have children, Jim?"

"Nope. Married and divorced years ago. You?"

"No. I've got a girlfriend, but she lives in Macon, and I only get to see her on weekends. Kind of a G-U relationship?"

"G-U?"

"Geographically Undesirable."

Jim chuckled. "G-U. I'll have to remember that. That's funny. What's her name?"

"Candy."

Jim closed the folder on the Coroner's Reports. "Go home Ryan. Go call Candy. Call your parents. See you back here tomorrow."

They walked to the elevator together, and then to the parking lot.

"Jim, can I ask you something?"

"Why did I choose you?"

"Yeah. I mean, you could have asked for a detective . . . someone with experience in this sort of thing. Why me?"

"Honestly, I didn't expect to be here more than a couple of days. Someone with experience would have likely opened a lot of doors I didn't think I needed to go through. I thought this would be a 'one and done' murder, and I'd fly home. Looks like I was wrong. But, I'm not sorry I chose you. You've been a big help. You make a mean cup of coffee."

Ryan watched the agent drive away. Jim had a room at the Peachtree Plaza. It was after seven and already dark in Atlanta. He could see the red swirling glow of the Coca Cola sign through the buildings. Ryan sat in his car resting his head on the steering wheel. After a few minutes, he unbuckled his seat belt and opened the door. He had to keep up. He had to do his part. Ryan walked back in the building and up the elevator to retrieve the report folder. He would go over every detail from the Coroner. He settled into his chair. It would be hours before he talked to Candy and even longer before he dared to face the shadowy demons in his sleep.

CR•ꝏ

Dear Crabigail,

My husband is about to retire soon from his job as an accountant. Can you suggest a good job for him post retirement?

Thanks,
Used to an Empty House

Dear Empty Headed,

When my own John Earl got hisself laid off from the cement mixing plant last week or so, I pretended to get him a job as a pollen counter for the Weather Channel. I give him an old shoe box and told him to stand hisself out in the front yard. He catches that yeller pollen all day, and then spends his evenings at the kitchen table separating and counting it. He asked me how he got paid for this, and I told him, he'd get paid per pollen. So, he's up to about seven billion right now, and I'm sitting in his recliner watching "Days of Our Lives," and eatin' rice crispy squares in peace.

Yers,
Crabigail

CR•ƎO

CHAPTER 11
PASS THE PEAS AND A THREE LEGGED TURKEY

The forecast for Thanksgiving could not have been more pleasant. My favorite weatherman and Dan's least favorite, who looks like a young Donny Osmond and wears sharp looking pin stripe suits, said it would be sunny and seventy-five. The cousins had been sending the usual back and forth bantering and trash talk texts over the inevitable wiffle ball game that would occur on the lawn between Mom's house and my brother, Brett's following a sumptuous turkey dinner.

They came from all over . . . Pam's three . . . Rebecca, Jennifer, and Jarrett with his wife, Amanda. Amanda was expecting and had that glowing look new mothers-to-be always had. Jarrett, the proud expecting papa, helped her out of the car. As Jennifer unloaded her car, her little boy, James ran up Mom's front steps to the landing and stood with an "I'm King of the World" stance waving a brand new plastic wiffle ball bat and announced "I am eight years old, and I'm old enough to play this year. I want to be on Jarrett's team." Jennifer sniffed at that, as she refused to play on her brother's side and pretended to be offended by her son's betrayal. James tugged on his Aunt Rebecca, who arrived earlier that morning with Pam, and quickly recruited her to his team.

"Also . . . " James said with grand emphasis.

I grabbed him from Rebecca for a quick hug.

"Also, what?"

"I claim the turkey leg!"

"Oh no you don't!" Jarrett and my son, Chris said this in unison.

Chris patted James on the head. "Too bad little boy. Jarrett and I claimed them last year for this year."

Jarrett stood his ground, too. "That's right, James. You aren't old enough to merit the coveted turkey leg. Chris and I have a long set precedence, and you can't change our Thanksgiving tradition."

James folded his arms in defiance. "That is not fair! I'm gonna ask Mammaw." But, he heard Rob, Brett's son call him from my brother's porch and ran to see him, instead. I knew James. He'd take up the argument later, most definitely with my mother. I didn't think Chris or Jarrett would actually deny him anyway, but they would make him earn that turkey leg.

I heard the booms of target shooting from Brett's back deck. Brett has quite the gun collection, and he and Rob enjoyed shooting at paper plates that traveled into place up the mountain on an elaborate pulley system my brother rigged.

My three had the furthest to travel. Meagan and her sweet husband, Jeff were coming from Lancaster, Pennsylvania. Leslie and her fiancé, David flew in the night before from Virginia. I was delighted that my son Chris had a rare month at home. He spent the last six months on a Viking Cruise Ship where he performed with girlfriend, Sarah, while traveling all over the world. They would fly to Africa and return to the ship after the holidays. Sarah flew in from a visit at her parent's home in Boston, and we picked her up at Atlanta Hartsfield Jackson Airport at the same time we fetched Leslie and David. We took two cars to accommodate everyone comfortably. Meagan and Jeff left the day before and planned to stop for the night on the highway. I wasn't sure if they were there yet.

We could see that Mom had gone to great lengths to set up extra tables and place settings. She had several long tables end to end on the porch, creating an L shape, connecting with the dining room table inside. Some lucky diner's chair would be both inside and outside.

I spotted my sister rocking away on the porch. Pam had her hands on her hips, signaling her normal snarky self. As I approached the house with my usual contribution to the occasion . . . a bag of Tupperware for take-homes, she yelled down at me.

"Nice of you to show up, after all the potatoes are peeled."

I looked up at her and smiled. "I hate peeling potatoes. You should know that. I buy the microwave kind."

"The horrors. How many microwaves have you gone through this year?"

"Just two. And I did make the sweet potato casserole. Dan has it."

Meagan and Jeff came from around the back of the house carrying some extra folding chairs. I squealed as I hugged their necks. I hadn't seen my eldest daughter and son-in-law in half a year. Leslie visits them often as they only live a couple of hours apart, so she and David gave quick hugs and walked over to Brett's to participate in the death of more paper plates. I couldn't help it. I jumped every time a gun fired. The sound echoed through the forest. I imagined every living creature that could fled from the booming gunshots. Mom's poor koi would be hiding under the rocks of the fish pond shaking to their gills.

Chris was getting hugged to death, first by Pam on the porch, and then by Mom, in the kitchen. I could hear her squeals from the driveway. Poor little Sarah was probably overwhelmed by it all, especially with the explosions of gun fire coming every few seconds just a hundred yards away.

Mom seemed oblivious to the ringing noise. "Chriiiiiiiiiiiiiis!!!! Lord help me. Just look at you!!! You've gone and grown muscles. And Sarah! So glad to have you both here and not captured by pirates."

The possibility of pirates was a constant fear of Mom's since the two of them sailed off on the high seas. She has a rather active imagination.

"Where's your mother? I needed her here an hour ago to peel potatoes. Poor Pam had to do them all by herself."

"I'm here, Mom. Sorry about the potatoes." I walked into the kitchen and kissed Mom on the cheek.

Mom ignored my half-hearted apology and thrust a cup of hot coffee in my left hand and the half and half in the other. I could hear Dan on the steps talking to Meagan and Jeff. He and Jeff were having a conversation about mileage and how long it took to drive from Pennsylvania and what routes they took. I have no idea why this is always important to men, but it is. As I took a sip of my coffee, I heard a fake cough and turned to find my cousin Sherry. This time it was my turn to squeal.

Mom calls Sherry "the triplet," because she loves her as much as us, and Sherry's feelings are reciprocal. We are very close in age, and though she's a gorgeous blonde and we are brunettes, Pam and I consider her more triplet sister than cousin. I had no idea she was coming this year, driving from her home in Tennessee, and I couldn't have been more delighted.

I sat at the indoor table and caught up with Sherry. Dan put my casserole dish of sweet potatoes in the oven and joined us. He pointed our attention out the window.

"What are they doing?"

I looked out across the driveway and saw Brett carrying an old-fashioned turntable. Behind him was Rob pushing two large speakers that were bungee corded to a dolly. Behind him was David with an even bigger speaker. Leslie followed with the matching speaker and an extension cord curled on top. Rebecca was directing them all and helping with placement. I shrugged.

"Who knows . . . Dinner music, maybe?"

I saw my great nephew James, hop down the stairs of Brett's house with a single vinyl album.

Brett yelled, "James, be careful. Don't drop it. It's the only one I have."

"I got this." James said this with an air of importance. His wiffle ball bat was tossed in the grass. Whatever was going on, he was in on it.

They didn't carry their burdens to Mom's house. They stopped, instead at the picnic pavilion in between. Not very many folks have a picnic pavilion in their front yards. My dad built it when, I guess, he couldn't think of anything else to build. The thing was huge enough that Brett now uses it to store two large boats. But, back in the day, back when Dad was alive, we had many a cookout down there. It even featured screened bins all around the edge so that Mom could safely put serving dishes of food out without fear of flies. For a country girl, my mother has an unnatural fear of flies touching her food.

We watched as the group set up the equipment on an old army surplus folding table Dad brought home from Vietnam. They positioned the speakers toward the road beyond and not toward us. Rebecca plugged the extension cord into the outdoor outlet. I just couldn't wait any longer. I walked out there.

"Brett, what are y'all doing?

"You'll see."

"You have the speakers turned backwards."

"No I don't."

I was about to ask more questions, but I could hear my Mom calling me to put ice in glasses, her universal signal that dinner was nearly ready. Everyone was there, Dan carved the turkey, and I could smell those heavenly home-made yeast rolls in their final moments of browning. We would be eating soon. I hurried back up the steps. Jennifer and Amanda were carrying serving bowls. Jeff was sneaking bits of turkey off the platter and getting playful smacks on the hand by Mom's spatula. The only thing missing was my dad.

James clanged the huge wrought iron dinner bell and everyone came to the half indoors and half outdoors arrangement of tables and took their seats. Jeff snagged the crossroads chair in the doorway. As usual, we left the seat closest to the kitchen free for Mom, though she hardly ever sat down during Thanksgiving. We fuss and fuss about it, but she always had one more pan of rolls in the oven and extra gravy to stir. She rarely sat until the rest of us were on second helpings, and she had no more excuses.

When my father was alive, he added much to the festivities of the occasion. Every year we would wait for it. Mom would lay out the most incredible feast. And every year, my dad would wait for prayers, and then ask for someone to pass him the peas, knowing full well that peas are the one vegetable my mother doesn't serve at Thanksgiving. Mom would tell him, "Frank, you know where the Le Sueurs are, and the can opener, and the microwave. Knock yourself out." This scene replayed year after year, to the amusement of everyone, until that last Thanksgiving five years ago, that we spent in the hospital dining room eating sliced compressed turkey and lumpy canned gravy, as we futilely waited for him to get better. The annual teasing of Mom wasn't possible with that big tube down his throat. I didn't think I would ever enjoy Thanksgiving again, after he died, but here we were and it was wonderful.

Mom's feast was abundant. Along with those heaven sent and scented yeast rolls and a huge turkey, were mashed potatoes, my sweet potato casserole with pecan coconut topping, macaroni and cheese, giblet gravy, both kinds of cranberries, pecan honey butter for the rolls, broccoli, green beans, Pam's fried okra, squash, and some kind of gelatin with marshmallow creation that I always skipped in favor of an extra roll, but the kids loved. Later, there would be a choice of French Coconut Pie or Chocolate Chip Pecan, both served warm with whipped cream on top. Most of us would have both. There would also be one pumpkin pie only Jeff would eat.

James again yelled that he wanted the turkey leg. Jarrett and Chris, with good natured older cousin aggression, told him that was not happening. To everyone's delight, Mom came from the kitchen with the turkey platter holding three massive turkey legs. There were lots of giggles and comments about the rare three-legged turkeys of Blue Ridge. We all filled our plates, but there would not be a bite taken until Mom delivered a proper prayer of thanks.

We settled back in our chairs. Our bodies were like tight wound springs as we waited on my Mom to bless the food and thank the good Lord. Our stomachs growled, triggered by incredible smells of delicious food.

"Y'all bow your heads."

We did, but you could feel the tension build as the aroma of the feast drifted all around us. We were hungry.

"Dear Heavenly Father, we thank you for this food and for every one that has gathered here . . . We ask that if it be your will, no one breaks a bone during wiffle ball . . . Also, if it be your will, we ask for safe travels for everybody. We are thankful for Sarah and Chris being protected by you from pirates on that big ocean . . . We thank you for the sweet baby girl that Amanda is carrying . . . We thank you for another great year and for extra turkey legs sold at Ingles. Amen."

"Amen!" We responded properly, and the springs were sprung. We reached for the serving spoons, but we had to abruptly wind ourselves back, because Mom had a PS to her prayer.

"PS LORD."

Someone, I think it was James, sighed out loud. Mom opened one eye and stared at him. I know this because I have a bad habit of peeking during any prayer.

"Lord we ask that you don't let that . . . you know who . . . do you know what . . . to Penny or Pam."

I guess since she already amened her prayer, she didn't feel like she could say it again. So instead, she came up with an original ending.

"That is, if it be your will. Thank you and . . . bye bye . . . Good night."

We all looked up and grinned. Rob broke the silence finally by saying, "That was awesome."

And it was. "Bye bye, goodnight" would, forever after, be our response to Mom's "Amen," a fact that embarrassed her to no end, and she would never be okay with, but that was just too bad.

We chowed down. Lively conversation and laughter trickled from the dining room and out the door, around the corner to the outdoor tables. Chris and Sarah told their cousins about racing each other on the original Olympic track in Greece. Sarah yelled at Chris to wait for her and he had. He stopped on the track so they could finish together. But, as they neared the finish line, Sarah shot ahead and beat him. Chris was good natured about all the ribbing he took for allowing his adorable girlfriend to outfox him. I decided right then to paint Sarah a fox for Christmas and Chris, a sadly, slow snail.

Leslie, a school teacher, asked Pam some questions about a student that she thought might be left-handed, but was using his right. Pam had seen pretty much everything in her thirty years of teaching.

Pam told Leslie to give the child a complicated math problem to work out in his head, and to watch whether he looked up to the right or up to the left while he calculated. This would tell her whether he was left or right dominant.

Brett, who knows something about everything, interrupted with a ridiculous tale about how he always chooses the right wing or the right breast from chickens or turkeys. This was because Brett felt like fowl had to be like humans, which meant most would be right-handed. And like humans, the right side would be used more and be more developed. Not one of us questioned the fact that turkeys don't even have hands.

Brett continued. "Why would I eat a measly A cup when I can have a C cup?"

Meagan coughed violently on that comment and had to be pounded on the back by Sherry.

Rebecca asked, "Excuse me. How do you know they're right-handed . . . or winged . . . or whatever?"

"Have you ever noticed that a chicken tilts its head to the left like right-handed humans?

Pam, the retired teacher of the blind, chimed in. "Well . . . actually . . . I've studied the reason that chickens tilt their heads to the left."

Rebecca rolled her eyes. "Really, Mom?

"I read a study while researching nystagmus. This is a condition where a person has rapid lateral eye movement, and this causes low vision. Researchers wondered why children with nystagmus tended to tilt their head to the left. They compared this tendency to chickens who all have nystagmus.

Meagan asked, "Are chickens blind?"

"No. They have functional vision, but it's impaired, so they are nearly blind. Anyway, it was determined that tilting the head improves visual acuity by slowing down the effects of nystagmus. Think of a level. When you tilt it, the liquid goes slanted, and you have to adjust to make it go straight. For a person or a chicken with nystagmus, crooked is straight."

Brett seemed to ponder this scientific truth for a moment. "Dang it. So because I keep my head straight, I might be eating the little boobs? That might be why the girl at KFC looked at me weird when I asked for the right breast."

Rob chuckled. "Dad, I'm pretty sure we all know why she looked at you weird."

Jeff, Dan, and David hardly said a word. They probably couldn't get a word in if they wanted to, so they just enjoyed their meal and ignored Gardin clan conversation.

All the while, Mom hovered bringing out more rolls. She would actually retrieve cold rolls from our plates, and substitute with hot ones, which we slathered with honey pecan butter. Finally, after much persuasion we convinced her to sit and join the feast.

Meagan changed the subject from chicken bra sizes by telling Pam how she had enjoyed her weekly Crabigail column. For those that hadn't read it, Meagan tried to repeat Pam's letter from a woman whose husband was retiring and wanted a suggestion on an appropriate second career. Crabigail answered back that she made her own husband become a pollen counter. There was no explanation as to how someone would count tiny specks of pollen, or what tools they would use.

Brett was then inspired to launch into another completely inappropriate dinnertime story.

"I know a guy who won a ten dollar bet by scraping up a line of pine pollen and snorting it. Now, pine pollen doesn't normally bother anyone, due to its size and weight, making it not as airborne as hardwood and other microscopic pollen. But apparently, snorting it in large quantities is a really bad idea, and ten bucks didn't come close to paying his out of pocket expenses for his little stay in the hospital."

Rob looked at his dad. "Please say that person wasn't you."

Brett ignored him. "By the way, another name for pollen is 'tree sperm.' This is a fun fact I like to bring up while people are complaining about choking on the stuff."

The conversation was interrupted by loud noises from rambunctious bicyclists making the curve down our road. Brett jumped up and raced down the steps, followed by Rob. The rest of us watched in amusement. We all knew that Brett despised the, as he called them, city hipster bicyclists that were riding by in a pack of six: three young men and three young women with backpacks filled with party supplies. He was familiar with this group. They irked him because they would act all Mother Nature until they got to the lake, but refused to carry off their trash or properly put out their campfires. Brett had seen them every Thanksgiving, and a week each spring and summer, for the last three years and knew they would once again show up. Brett was sick and tired of cleaning up their messes. This time he was ready for them.

When Brett got to the pavilion, he started the record. After the initial crackle the "Dueling Banjo" theme song to "Deliverance" radiated loud enough to more than reach the road and beyond. I guess the bicyclists, despite their young ages, had seen the movie, because they stopped on the curve just before the perpetual pot hole and talked amongst themselves. They looked our way. I'm sure they could see the odd table sticking out of the door and the stretch of tables beyond. I watched their heads turn to the right where they spotted my brother and his son. Carbon copies those two, standing by the pavilion with hands on hips. Both big and powerful looking with matched balding heads tilted to the left and shotguns on their shoulders. Rob was the young ogre in training. The six talked some more and then, with uneasy glances at one another, turned their bikes around and headed back down the way they had come.

Mom shook her head as Brett and Rob stowed the empty shotguns back in the pavilion and returned to the table.

"Brett! What will those people think?"

"Well, Mom . . . every other idea I had turned out to be felonies."

Mom's lips were still pursed in disapproval. "Brett Gardin, I'm ashamed of you." But, we knew she wasn't. Like Brett, she despised litterers. She handed him another hot roll and the bowl of honey pecan butter. I smiled and gave my own silent prayer, thanking God for my crazy family, and as always, I wished my dad was there. Thank You and Goodnight.

CR•ED

Dear Crabigail,

Can you recommend ways to spice up my marriage? My husband seems bored.

Signed,
Shy in Shenandoah

Dear Shy Shmy,

Ya know that store, Victoria's Secret? Well drive right on past it, cause anything they sell there won't fit ya, or yer husband wouldn't be bored. Whatcha ort to do is take up pole dancing. So, drive right on past that Victoria's Secret to the nearest bait and tackle shop. Buy yer husband a brand new fishing pole. Then stick a bunch of them sticky fishing lures all over yer girly parts, and when he comes home, dance around that fishing pole. He'll be so excited to see that new pole, he won't even notice yer flabby parts and stretch marks. If that don't excite him, then at least he'll go fishing on Saturday while you ketch up on one of them trashy novels.

Yers,
Crabigail

⊱•⊰

CHAPTER 12
COFFEE GROUNDS IN MY CUP

Mom called at seven am. I was ready for her and, for once, already had my coffee cup filled and in my hand.

"Morning, Mom."

"Listen! I want you to drive up to Rome and pick up Pam again and then go to the police station and turn yourselves in."

Dang it! There were grounds floating in my coffee. I hate when I get grounds on the other side of the filter. The floaters are almost impossible to remove. I used my finger with learned skill and skimmed the side of the cup. The grounds clung to my finger, and I was able to flick them into the sink.

"What crime did we commit, Mom?"

"I didn't say you committed a crime. You can confess to whatever you want."

More grounds floated to the top, and I continued my coffee exorcism. I refused to take a sip until I had them all out, but I badly needed the caffeine.

"And, we would confess to a crime we didn't do for what reason?"

"Haven't you been watching the news? There is a serial killer running around, and he is killing TWINS!"

I had indeed seen the news, and I knew that's what she was calling about, and I knew that she would call first thing that morning. Another set of twins had been found murdered in Atlanta the day before.

"Lots of twins in the world, Mom. I'm sure we are down the totem pole of expected victims."

I made a third swoop of my cup and could see I was making progress.

"That's a terrible analogy. Why are you bringing Indians into it?

"I don't know, Mom. Maybe because it is seven in the morning, and I haven't had coffee yet."

"I just don't understand why you and Pam aren't a bit worried. YOU ARE TWINS!"

More grounds floated up. Plan B. I took a napkin out of the cabinet and placed it over a bowl. I poured the coffee from my cup over my make-do filter. Apparently, my napkins are not very porous, because, instead of soaking through and capturing the grounds, the coffee pooled up and ran all over the counter. My morning was not starting well.

"I'm aware that we are twins, Mom. But the murderer is in Atlanta, not Carrollton or Rome. Hopefully there are enough twins in the big city to give him years of enjoyment before he feels the need to head West on I-20."

"Listen to me, and listen good. You and your sister have gotten sort of famous. And now, your sister has that column in the papers that everyone is reading and talking about, and she's very vulnerable. I think this killer will come after one of you or the two of you. I want you both safe. Locked up behind bars with lots of police around should do it."

I wiped up the coffee from the counter and the floor and the front of my dishwasher. Then, I poured the whole pot of coffee down the sink, rinsed it out, and started over with a fresh and properly placed filter. I sure did miss my percolator and made a mental promise to check Amazon for a new one.

"How about a compromise, Mom? How about if I drive to Rome and pick Pam up and bring her here again? At least we will get murdered together."

"That's not in the least bit funny, but do it. Oh, and I need you to make the sweet potatoes again for Thanksgiving next year. They were delicious"

I shook my head as I returned the wall phone to its cradle. Dan called from the living room.

"Who was that?"

"Who do you think it would be this early?"

"Hmmm. Speaking of early, I hear Chris up already." Our son was home for a visit between acting gigs.

"Yeah. He has an audition in Atlanta this morning. I have to drive to Rome and get Pam again, and please remember that I have to make the sweet potatoes A YEAR FROM NOW. I know my voice rose at the end like I was on my last nerve.

"You sound like you need coffee."

"That would be a big fat yes."

Dan tilted his head. He was listening to the coffee pot gurgling. "What are you doing in there? I made a fresh pot, already."

"Had grounds in it."

My mood was slipping into pure grumpiness, so I took the pot off of the Mr. Coffee and sat it on a dry dish towel. I placed my cup in its place, and because this wasn't my first rodeo, held the spring up so that the brew would continue to drip right into my cup.

"Mom wants me to pick up Pam so we can get murdered together."

"Sounds like a plan."

"Murdered? Who's getting murdered?" Chris barreled down the stairs.

I didn't answer my son, and it didn't matter. He was already chatting with his dad about the weather and traffic alerts that would be covered in great detail on the morning news. It didn't take either one of them long to forget all about me, and the fact that I might die at the hands of a serial killer or lack of caffeine.

My husband was full of sage advice. "If I were you I'd skip the gut and take 285."

"Yeah, but, then I have to deal with all those big trucks."

"That's true, but look at 75. Spaghetti junction is a mess."

I tuned them both out. Three fourths full, I removed my cup and returned the pot to its platform. I added a large dollop of heavy whipping cream. The fat free half and half in the door of the fridge would only have been sufficient if the day had started well, but it hadn't. I didn't stir as I always prefer to let the crean meander its way artistically through my cup on the natural path it would choose. As I lifted the cup to my lips, I could see the caramel and ecru swirls begin to settle into a galactic pattern. Steam rose, and I took the first sip. I closed my eyes and smiled.

I opened my eyes with a gasp. Did I leave my four inch deep glass casserole at Mom's the week before? The one I brought the sweet potatoes in? The one with the lid with the sculptured round knob? I use that dish all the time. I sat my coffee on the counter and opened the door to the garage to check my storage cabinet. As I stepped out I felt myself plunge into nothingness. I screamed.

Dan's mother lived in an assisted living facility around the corner from our neighborhood until her passing in January. Years before, I built a six-inch high wooden step to make it easier for Nancy . . . Nannee to the grandchildren . . . to climb the steep twelve inches from garage to kitchen. For some unearthly reason, Dan decided that very morning that the step was no longer necessary. However, he forgot to tell me.

Expecting a step that was not there, I fell forward. Flailing at the empty air, I managed to grasp the small cabinet to the right that we used for storing wine. Instead of helping though, it tipped forward and bottles of Malbec flew with me to the concrete floor.

In a mixture of red wine and glass my body skidded forward, so that my head went under Dan's car and behind the front wheel. Hearing my scream and the crash, Chris was the first to reach the doorway.

"Oh, no. Oh, my God. Mom!" he screamed.

I learned later that, from Chris' view, he couldn't see my head behind the car wheel and due to the red wine, he thought he was seeing the headless corpse of his mother laying in a pool of blood.

"Go . . . and . . . get . . . your . . . Dad!"

Chris screamed again. He thought my severed head was speaking to him.

"How did you get all the way up under my car?" Dan pulled me by my ankles and helped me up, amazed that I wasn't cut by the glass. I was however, covered in red wine and in a few hours, I would be stove up all over by the fall. I looked at them both.

"Where . . . is . . . my . . . step?"

"Um. I didn't think we still needed it. Guess I was wrong."

"You think?" I glared. "I shall take a shower now . . . WITH my coffee, and go to Pam's. Whoever thought removing my step was a good idea can clean this up."

"It was Dad."

"Sorry."

I looked at my son. "And YOU! . . . All your cruise ship first aid training couldn't have helped me any better than you just 'oh my God-ding' in the doorway? Taking the Lord's name in vain!"

"I'm sorry too, Mom." He had the nerve to giggle. "We didn't cover decapitations."

I stomped past them both, stopping at the counter to retrieve my properly brewed, groundless coffee. I continued on to the shower, not really mad, but also not caring that red wine was dripping from my bangs to the end of my nose and into my precious cup of coffee.

ᘓ•ᘔ

Dear Crabigail,

My husband is being forced to retire following a massive heart attack. I know I should be more sympathetic, but I'm used to having the house to myself and can't stand the thought of him puttering around here all day. Does that make me an awful wife?

Heartfelt in Hiram

Dear Heartless,

Yes, but who the hell cares. You don't want him sitting around all day wolf whistling at Vanna and guessing the Wheel of Fortune puzzles just before you do. Just do like I did and convince him his pacemaker is solar powered, so he'll have to stay outside all day to keep it charged up.

Yers,
Crabigail

☙ • ❧

CHAPTER 13
PHENOPHOTO WHAT?

Ryan was sitting in his now customary chair on the visitor's side of the worn metal desk reading FBI reports and writing information in his spiral notebook when Jim walked in. Jim could see the Coroner's reports sticking out from the newer documents he had asked Ryan to examine. Without a word, he dropped another file on top of the documents in Ryan's lap.

"What's this?"

"DNA reports. We have both semen and touch DNA, and we've run them through the system. They don't have a match on anyone, but might still be useful.

"How? Like when we catch him?"

"Well there's that, but DNA has other uses, too."

Ryan was fascinated. "How so?"

Jim took his seat on the other side of the desk, wiping an empty cracker wrapper into the overflowing dented wastebasket below. He and Ryan had noted before that it was uncanny how the desk, the concrete walls, the off-by-an-hour clock on the wall, and the wastebasket came in the exact same ugly peeling shade of greenish-gray paint. Their hard wooden chairs had years of dried crud nestled between the slats. The Atlanta Police Department had gone all out on accommodations for the visiting FBI agent and his rookie partner.

"Phenotyping. We have folks who can delve into the markers of the DNA and determine features of the perp. We can, for starters, determine the race of the individual."

"That's helpful."

"By itself it isn't much." Jim opened a new pack of peanut butter Nekots. "But, technology is a wonderful thing. DNA takes us a lot further now. We can phenotype, which means we can use computer analysis to pull genetic information and create a molecular photofit."

"I . . . what? What is that?"

Jim poured a fresh cup of coffee from the, once white, coffee maker that hadn't had a good cleaning in a long time. He took a sip.

"Good coffee, Ryan. We can actually create a rough photograph of the killer using his molecular DNA."

"No freaking way."

"We should have something soon. We already know he's white and blond-headed.."

"This is like something out of the movies. Does it really work?"

"It does. It's a pretty good tool. Pulling apart this guy's DNA will give us an idea of who we are looking for."

"Man, oh man. That's awesome. When?"

"Patience, Ryan. Takes some time. I'll let you know when I know."

"Man, oh man."

Ryan opened the file and began reading. None of it made any sense to him. He tried to take notes, but it was like trying to dictate a conversation with a Martian. He found his eyes glazing over.

Jim laughed. "You have no idea what you're reading. Give me that back." He laughed some more and topped off his coffee, finishing the pot.

That stung a little, but Ryan shrugged it off, and handed the file to the detective. "Do you understand what's in here?"

"Nope. Makes my eyes tired to look at it. Something else, I need to run over with you."

"Okay?"

"I've got a courier bringing a letter over from the Sheriff from Dekalb County. Seems like our guy may be writing letters to future victims."

Ryan sat up straight. "If he is, that's pretty dumb."

"I think so, too. Still it's a lead. So far they've rounded up letters . . . threatening letters . . . from a dozen sets of twins. Living twins. I expect there will be more."

Jim tossed the half pack of Nekots to Ryan.

Selecting a cracker, Ryan could only say, "Man, oh man."

CR•ಏ

Dear Crabigail,

Last week I arrived at my fiancé's house an hour earlier than I was supposed to. I rang his doorbell and waited and waited. Then, I heard some scuffling on the side of the garage where he had a ladder leaning. I saw this naked blond climbing down, and my fiancé was tossing her clothes out the window. Heartbroken, I ran to my car, threw my engagement ring out the window, called them every name I could think of, backed into his Ferrari, and drove to a bar and got drunk. I need your help deciding if I should have done something different.

Signed,
Broken Hearted in Baton Rouge

Dear Broken,

You got yerself a boatload of should've, could've, would've. So, I'll jest answer one problem. Folks need to be careful climbing down them ladders. My own John Earl tried to climb one to patch the hole in our roof. Before he got hisself to the gutters, he started teetering and teetering til he dropped his whole box of nails, six shingles, a claw hammer and a six pack of Pabst Blue Ribbon. Durn near hit me in the head. So, I like to let folks know to stay off them ladders. You can pass that on to yer feller and his girlfriend.

Yers,
Crabigail

CS•ED

CHAPTER 14
WHEN YOU THINK YOU'VE HEARD EVERYTHING

Around seven in the morning, Mom made her daily call to make sure Pam and I hadn't been murdered in the night and to let me know that Blue Ridge was under a weather advisory with tornado warnings. Once she was assured we were alive, she started venting about a leak in her koi pond, which led to a vent about my brother, Brett. Somewhere in the middle of the story, she had me looking at her Facebook post about a snake on the front porch. While I was looking for the post, she requested that I stop and send her my recipe for Three Wise Men Sausage Bites. I was to type it in an email and send it to her with a picture of what they should look like. Conversations with Mom are often multitask layers of activity.

"Brett gets aggravated because I say 'water pond.' He says all ponds have water. That's the very definition of a pond, and I should just say 'pond' and stop being redundant. Did you find the recipe yet? But I like to say 'water pond,' and I'm not apologizing for it. Bring up Facebook again on your computer. I want you to like my story about the snake on the porch. Where's Pam? Lord! That wind is howling outside."

I had the phone on speaker and was able to half listen as I searched for her Facebook post about the snake on her porch. Snakes on Mom's porch aren't that unusual and, quite frankly, not that interesting. Snakes in early December were odd though, but it had been an especially warm fall, and I guess the reptiles were happily staying above ground. Still, I promised to look and finally found it. What caught my eye wasn't the post itself, but a comment from LaVon, a high school classmate. Growing up, LaVon was called "Bon" by Mom and her friends for a reason no one could remember. She was my mother's best friend. Bon had written, "This reminds me of one of the short stories you used to write, Betty. I remember you couldn't tell fact from fiction."

Short stories? This was news to me . . . I interrupted Mom's vent just as she was getting to the part where her next door neighbor friend Gloria agrees that "waterpond" is a perfectly acceptable word and resisted the immediate urge to point out that "water pond" is two words, Mom . . . "MOM!"

"What? Don't tell me you agree with your brother."

"No. It's the comment I just read on Facebook from Bon about your snake on the porch. What's the deal about you writing short stories? I've never heard this before and I thought by now I knew everything there was to know about my mother."

"I wrote poetry, too."

"Get out of here! I want to read them."

"No. They don't exist anymore, and I don't remember a one of them."

There was a long pause as we both listened to Mom's weather radio update. A tornado had touched down in Blairsville about thirty miles from her. Then she said, "There's something else you don't know about me."

"What is that?"

"I was in a play in high school, too. It was my senior year."

"WHAT?"

"Sure was. It was called *Where's Grandma?* I played the mother. It was the lead role."

She went on to tell me backstage and onstage stories about her experience. I was fascinated. All of these years coming to her grandchildren's productions, and she never mentioned it. While she talked, I managed to finish copying and pasting the Three Wise Men Sausage Bite recipe, with a large colorful picture of the hors d'oeuvre, into an email and hit send.

"Mom, that is amazing. Your recipe should be in your inbox, and I do want you to write down some of those stories. Remember, you have to buy sausage with sage in it like Jimmy Deans. It's the sage that makes 'em wise. Hey, they have extended your tornado warning another hour. I just saw it on Channel 2 and . . ."

"Have you ever known me to NOT buy sage sausage? I have a weather radio, and I can't remember any of those stories. I do remember that I wrote something every day, though. I had this mean teacher in seventh grade named Mr. J M Rutherford, Jr. I couldn't stand the man. If one kid in the class misbehaved, he made every one of us miss recess. How fair is that?"

On that point, I was sympathetic. "It's not fair, Mom. I can't stand when teachers do that. It punishes the whole group instead of the guilty." I had no idea where she was going with this new turn in the conversation.

"Exactly! Anyway, I don't know why I did it because, as I said, I just didn't like him at all. He was mean. Nevertheless, every day when I walked by him to leave for my next class, I would slide a piece of paper out of my notebook and lay it on his desk. It would be a poem or a short story that I had written that morning. By the way, I do buy hot sometimes."

"Nope. Sage, only. Wow! What did he say?"

"Not a word . . . ever . . . and they weren't for a grade, either. Not sure why I did it."

"I think it's wonderful. I hope he read them."

"Years later, when your dad and I moved back with you girls from Alaska . . . we were visiting family in Tennessee. We had gone over to a little diner for lunch . . . had you girls all dressed up cute. You were about three I think . . . long, blond ringlets . . . matching pink dresses with rick-racked daisies on the front. You kept that blond hair until you were around eight. I'm glad Sherry still has hers. She'll love those sausage bites."

My mother can always remember what Pam and I wore on any occasion. She made many of our childhood clothes herself on her old Singer Sewing Machine that she still has.

"Anyway, this old lady came over to our table. I didn't think anything about it at first. You twins always attracted attention."

Mom had my rapt attention.

"The lady said 'You won't remember me, but I'm your teacher, Mr. Rutherford's widow. I just wanted you to know that you gave him a lot of joy in his last few years of teaching. He brought home every poem and short story that you wrote and read them out loud to me. He saved them all. He just loved them.'"

I gasped. "That's wonderful."

"I was so touched," Mom continued. "I wish now that I had thought to ask her for them back. I guess I didn't care enough at the time to think they would matter fifty something years later. I don't suppose their children saved them. I don't even know if they had children. My email just pinged. I got your recipe."

"Mom! That is an incredible story. It really is."

"I'll tell you something else . . . Oh. Nice picture . . . When I got to high school, I discovered a deep respect for old Mr. Rutherford. He was strict, but he taught me how to study. No other teacher did that. They didn't care enough to challenge us. The study skills I learned in seventh grade carried me through high school and made me a good student. I have Mr. J M Rutherford, Jr., to thank for that."

"Mom, please try your best to remember some of the stories you wrote or the poems. Do it for your grandchildren."

"I don't remember things like I used to."

"Well, you have to dig deep in your brain and retrieve them. Write me a story."

"No. That's your talent not mine . . . and don't say 'dig in your brain' it makes me think of that serial killer and the things he does to twins. Whatever talent I had back in the day is long gone."

"Mom, you are holed up waiting out tornado warnings. Grab a piece of paper and a pen and write me a story. Please!

"I guess I could tell you about that time I caught the groundhog with my bare hands. I remember that day. It had just rained and . . . ."

"NO! Don't tell me. Write it down! Please."

"I can't think to do that. The wind is ferocious outside. I think Gloria just lost a tree on the big hill."

"WRITE IT DOWN, MOM. STAY SAFE, and I'll check on you later. BYE!"

I hung up the phone on her before she could protest any more. Last thing I heard was her yelling, "YOU be safe! There's a serial killer out there."

CR•ßO

Dear Crabigail,

I think my husband has the seven year itch. He came home with a new sports car, and has started wearing cologne that I didn't buy him. What should I do?

Sincerely,
Still Willing To Scratch His Itch in Memphis

Dear Itchin and Bitchin,

I got that seven year itch one time, and thought it'd never clear up. Got it right on the left butt cheek right below that loose saggy skin where I couldn't reach it. I'd be at the Hoggly Woggly grocery store and start itching so bad, I'd have to run over to the meat section and rub up and down on some frozen streak o lean. I don't think a new car's gonna help yer husband though, what with all that soft leather. So git yerself over to the Hoggly Woggly and buy the poor man a nice frozen rump roast.

Yers,
Crabigail

CR•ƆO

CHAPTER 15
THIRD SHIFT

Vivien checked the IPhone in her uniform pocket. She wasn't waiting on a call but looked frequently at the time.

"Ten more minutes," she thought. She looked out of the third floor window of her patient's room, pressing down on the closed blinds. She could see the Coca Cola building a block away. The lights were beautiful in downtown Atlanta.

Ten minutes later, as if a bell had gone off on the precise second of two a.m., Nurse Rhonda poked her head in the door of room 312, and told Vivien she was going on break.

Vivien smiled. *Finally*, she thought, but what she said was, "Sure, take your time." She scribbled notes on Ms. Watkin's chart and waited another minute to be sure Rhonda had gone downstairs to the cafeteria. She had a little less than thirty minutes before Rhonda returned. No other staff worked the late shift on their floor. There was just no need.

"Good night, Ms. Watkins. Sleep tight."

Like all of her patients, Ms. Watkins didn't, couldn't reply back.

Vivien turned off the light, and as she walked through the doorway and into the corridor, she unbuttoned the top button of her uniform. At the nurses' desk, she spread the corners of the lapels apart so that a peach colored lacy bra teased around the edges. Then she reached behind the desk for her coffee cup. In the small breakroom, she filled the cup with water and heated it in the microwave like she often did for tea, but this time she didn't add a teabag. Instead, she carried the cup into Room 316 and put it carefully on the nightstand. Her patient opened his eyes.

He couldn't speak, but his eyes watched her like they did every night she visited. One corner of his mouth lifted a slight bit in the chiseled gorgeous face, and Vivien considered that to be a smile.

"Like what you see, you handsome man?"

Vivien lifted his hand and put it inside her opened dress, sliding his fingers under the lace and around her breast. His hands were soft from years of lying still in the hospital bed. Vivien moved his hand in a circular motion and moaned. She threw back her head and unclasped her long brunette hair, so that it fell around her shoulders. She unbuttoned another button, and then used her own hand to help his fingers squeeze together on her nipple. She couldn't be loud. Not here in the hospital. So, she bit her lip to try and stifle the moaning. It didn't work.

Vivien felt the familiar burning and aching between her legs. She was wet there, and so she used her other hand to slide her panties down and off. As she bent to get them from around her ankles she kissed his lips softly at first and then with a hard thrust of her tongue into his mouth. Vivien pulled the sheet down and lifted his gown.

"Nice," she said. You're ready for me I see." She winked at him and smiled and then moved his hand to the other breast. She thought she heard him make a noise. That would be a first. It was a small noise like a gasp.

"Just you wait, handsome man. I have a little surprise for you tonight."

Vivien took the cup of hot water and took a large sip. She held the water in her mouth for a full minute before swallowing. Her mouth, now extremely warm, slid down over his penis. She moved up and down, massaging his testicles tickling the ridges with her tongue. Another gasp. This time she was sure of it.

She looked into his eyes. They were dark and burning with desire. Vivien climbed onto the bed and straddled him. His penis slid easily into her vagina and filled her up. She could feel it press against her G spot tingling and volcanic. She moved slowly up and down, back and forth. They came together.

Exhausted, Vivien climbed off and used a dry washcloth to clean herself up. She tossed it into a Ziploc bag, sealed it, and placed it in her pocket. Then she wet another cloth and used it to wash him off. That one she tossed into the linen bag by the bathroom. She straightened her clothes, pulled his gown down, and the sheet up. Before she left the room, as she had for the last eight years of her employment at the Peachtree Rehabilitation Hospital, Vivien kissed the little scarred spot on his forehead . . . Adam's scar . . . where the nail had gone in so many years before.

CR•ƧO

Dear Crabigail,

No matter how careful I am, I always seem to have silly accidents, and I am such a klutz. How can I be more graceful?

Sincerely,
Calamity Jane

Dear Band-Aid covered Jane,

I got me a twin sister who acts jest like you, so I know how miserable all yer kin folk must be. Yer klutzy crap hurts them more than it does you. Did they ever wind up in yer vehicle, sideways in a swamp, staring at a sign that says, "PLEASE DON'T FEED THE GATORS!?" Did they ever get stuck standing out in the rain after a Conway Twitty concert, cause you locked yer keys in the trunk? Did they ever have to push yer car three miles up hill, cause you thought that E on the gas gauge meant Excellent? Well that's called the BAD CARMA. There's only one way to get good CARMA and that's to do a good deed for yer sister like buy her a gift certificate for a fancy restaurant like the Golden Corral or treat her to a pedicure so she can git them big toe nails she can't reach clipped. Better yet, next time she needs a ride to the Hoggly Woggly, send her an UBER!

Yers,
Crabigail

C•ʃ૭

CHAPTER 16
UNHANGING WITH LIZZIE

While Pam sat at my kitchen table working on her Dear Crabigail column, I left to spend a grueling day at Lizzie's helping her strip old, dated, flowery wallpaper off of her massive kitchen walls. The work wasn't what made it hard. I actually liked that part, and felt great success with each piece I successfully removed. What made the process awful was listening to the constant ping of Lizzie's phone as men on her match.com app sent her messages. Then, I would have to stop what I was doing, look at their pictures, and listen as Lizzie described them.

"This one lives in Hiram. His name is Man Without a Dog. He's okay looking, and he likes to hike and play Trivial Pursuit."

"Mmm-Hmm."

"He says, '*Hi, Scarlett. Read your profile. You look hot. Would you be interested in meeting up?*'"

"Tell him you look hot, because it is ninety degrees outside, and you are on top of a ladder. Anyone would look hot under that circumstance."

Lizzie ignored my snippy comment.

"Should I reply and meet up with him?"

"No."

"We'll see. I just might. I'm gonna keep him on my list of possibilities."

My best friend didn't have to look at me to know I was rolling my eyes. Lizzie's dedication to match.com was simply a way for her to deal with the loneliness and depression that followed the loss of the love of her life nearly two years before. She hated being alone in the huge house that she refused to part with. Her husband, Jim, a prominent Family Court Judge, died suddenly of a ruptured aorta due to a blood clot. He'd died about ten feet from where I was stripping wallpaper. Dan and I saw them a couple of hours before at an art exhibit opening. At home, Lizzie was finishing a bath while Jim made himself a cocktail. She found him collapsed on the sofa a few minutes later and, though she tried CPR, she knew immediately that it was hopeless. I found out on Facebook late that night when Lizzie returned alone from the Emergency Room and posted *"He's gone and the ice isn't even melted in his glass yet."*

Lizzie had no intention of dating any of the men she "met" on match. But, the connection, the constant connection, seemed to help lift her spirits some, and so I never really criticized. But, Lord a mercy, there were some nut jobs on there.

Ping

"Listen to this one!"

"Do I have to?"

"Afternoon, Scarlett. U look a lot like my diseased wife."

"I think he means 'deceased,'" she giggled.

"Lord."

Lizzie continued reading. *"I love your curly red hair. Could we meet for dinner? And would u be offended if I touched your hair? I'll wash my hands first."*

I was horrified. "Seriously! Delete him, right now."

Lizzie giggled again. I saw her swipe at her phone and prayed she had taken my advice. For at least five minutes, she actually worked a little. She managed to get a small piece of wallpaper down from over the doorway, during the time that I finished a 4x8 foot area near the dining table.

Ping

"Hey, Penny! This guy's match name is L-I-M-B, LIMB. I wonder if he's missing an arm or a leg. It says he's a veteran. Maybe he stepped on a landmine."

"Yeah, maybe. Or maybe L-I-M-B stands for 'Lives In Mom's Basement.' Fact is, Lizzie, you don't know the truth of anything those men post on there."

"I know. I just enjoy chatting with them. LIMB says he likes Disc Golf. I do, too! I might invite him to play one day on the Greenbelt Course."

"Really? Since when do you play Disc Golf?"

"You think you know everything about me, but you don't."

Lizzie climbed down from her ladder and opened the pantry closet. "Come here and look."

I walked over and peered inside and was surprised to see a complete Frisbee set beside boxes of rice and pasta. Like golf clubs, they came in all sizes to match the distance or task a player required.

"Wow! When did you buy these?"

"I've been collecting them for a while. I first bought Patrick a set for his thirty-fifth birthday. I thought my son would enjoy playing with some of his friends. As I learned more about them, I decided to get a set for myself, too.

"That sounds like fun. Let's go play after we finish your kitchen."

"Seriously? You would play with me? I would love that and you can share . . ."

Ping

" . . . my Frisbees. I don't think it's necessary for you to buy . . ."

Lizzie froze as she stared at her phone. Her face went from its usual freckled pink to a ghastly grey. Then she held the phone to her chest and stared at me.

"Lizzie! What's wrong?"

Lizzie shook her head and looked at her phone again. She blinked and flinched like she was trying to unsee what was there.

"Let me see."

She reached to hand me the phone. I had to pull it from her grasp as if she didn't really want me to look.

"*Dear Scarlett*," I read aloud. "*I'm sure you are a lovely person, but it is your friend Penny I would really like to meet.*

And because, I'm in to double dating, you can invite her sister, Pam, too. Sweet, witty, Pam. I'd like to take them over your homemade step ladder at the barbed wire fence and into the pasture behind your house and take my pretty little knife and slit them both from gullet to pubis. That rickety old leafless tree just beyond your fence would make a nice spot for this, don't you think? Could you set that up for me? Maybe spread a blanket there? I'll be in touch on a date and time."

There was a generic silhouette where the picture of the writer would normally be. The faceless messenger was named *Double Date Dave*.

Without speaking, we dropped our wallpaper scrapers, grabbed our purses, and ran to Lizzie's Lexus in the garage. Lizzie nearly hit the garage door pulling out, and had to brake suddenly to allow the door to finish its ascent. We weren't going to the disc golf range that day, and we sure weren't going to finish the work in her kitchen. We were going straight to the police. I needed to call Pam and Dan, but I was shaking too hard to operate my phone. I would call them after I calmed down, if that moment ever came. I clutched my purse tightly against my breast like it was protective armor, and sat without speaking as Lizzie drove. For once, I didn't comment on her driving as she raced at high speed around the curving Blandenburg Road and into town.

❧•❧

Dear Crabigail,

My boyfriend is a Taurus, but I'm a Libra. Should I marry him?

Your Friend,
Bull Lover

Dear I Call Bull,

First of all put down that dang Horror Scope cause it don't mean diddly squat! Wanna know if yer man is worth marrying? Here's what you do. Start telling him some gossip you heard down at the Hoggly Woggly, like Beulla's done got herself knocked up by the gas meter reader, and her husband's about to git paroled, and she's trying to figure out how to make him think it's his, and so she says how she just wanted to wait until he got out before she had it, and he's too stupid to know a woman can't be pregnant fer seven years. Anyways, if you tell him that, and he seems real interested, and asks a lot of questions, then he's gay, and you don't want to marry him. If he gits real mad, and calls Beulla trashy names, then he's a bully, and you best kick him to the curb. But if his eyes glaze over, and he just nods and says, "that's real nice,"' then you know you got a normal man and you orta snap him up quick before Beulla does.

Yers, Crabigail

CR•ဆ

CHAPTER 17
SHEMAL

I was crammed into a tiny, overly warm office at the Police Station with Dan, Pam and Lizzie, as well as various police officers who came and went. We were there for hours. A woman detective made screenshot copies of the message and downloaded it from Lizzie's phone. I answered questions as best I could, with an upholstery spring poking me behind my kneecap. I made note that my next fundraiser would be for new chairs for the Carrollton Police Department. At one point they took Lizzie away and questioned her in another room. After about thirty minutes, they let her rejoin us in the cramped office.

Then the door opened, and in walked the handsomest man I've ever seen. He was very tall and black and gorgeous, and he was about our age. He had Rhett Butler's swarthiness including a wisp of hair over the forehead, Clint Eastwood's wrinkled brow and shuttered eyes, Kirk Douglas' cleft chin, and bronze flawless skin like Denzel Washington, not that I notice things like that. The man had the broad shoulders of a linebacker. Dan thinks I don't watch football when we go to Bobby Dodd Stadium to tailgate Georgia Tech games and that my ticket is wasted. I agree that I don't watch much, and usually bring a book to read. However, I do check out those linebackers in between chapters. This man could be a linebacker.

Pam tightened, and then leaned forward. "Shemar," she whispered.

I was so embarrassed. Pam loves Shemar Moore. He plays Derek Morgan on the TV show Criminal Minds, and Pam has said a million times how much she crushes on him. I don't watch the show, but I've seen enough to know she wasn't far off on the similarity. Still . . . Who says that out loud?

"I'm Agent Jim Candor with the FBI, and I'd like to go over this message with you if you don't mind." Agent Candor, notified of the warning on Lizzie's phone, had driven himself to the Carrollton precinct from Atlanta.

"Sure, Yes, Okay." We all murmured different things.

"First, I want to assure you that we have agents and officers on watch at your home. I would prefer you not go anywhere without accompaniment until we catch this guy. Second, we have reason to believe that these messages are not from the killer, but someone who reads the paper and is having a little fun of their own."

I took note of the plural: *messages*. "So there are others?"

"Yes. Yours makes the fourteenth such letter. No one that has received a letter has been victimized, nor do we have any reason to believe they will. But, we'll take precautions to keep you safe."

He looked at Lizzie. "Ma'am, I understand the description of your backyard is pretty accurate? The fence, the tree, the steps? We have a photographer there now taking pictures."

Speechless, Lizzie nodded.

Agent Candor looked at Pam and me. "I know this is an unusual request, but the FBI task force is bringing together some of the twins who received notes to D.C. for a few days. They want to conduct some tests and questionnaires to see if you have information that could help us with the case. Would you be interested in coming? Ms. Pam, I understand you have some special skills that might be of use."

Like Lizzie, Pam was tongue-tied and couldn't answer, but I could. "We'd love to help."

Dan nodded. "I think that might be a good, safe place for you both to be right now. I say Go."

Pam finally spoke. "Shemar."

Agent Candor didn't seem to notice, or he'd heard it before and chose to ignore it. "I'll arrange a flight for early next week if that's not too soon."

I felt Pam tighten beside me again, but for a totally different reason. I knew we were going to have an issue. For all of Pam's bravery, she had a debilitating fear of flying. I'd deal with that later.

Agent Candor smiled. "Go home now, and we'll be in touch. I have an officer following you to your house and conducting surveillance around the clock. Ms. Lizzie, if you want to return to your own home, we'll have someone looking out for you, as well.

Lizzie nodded. She looked as starstruck as Pam. "Okay," she whispered. That was all Lizzie could get out. Normally, she would be bubbling over with chatter. I didn't know if it was nerves or attraction or what. I figured it was most likely the latter.

Lord.

ɐ•ɔ

Dear Crabigail,

I'm stuck at home with a husband who is the loudest eater I have ever known. Crackers and chips are bad enough, but the worst is cereal. He likes Grape Nuts. When he chews, every nerve I have is yelling at me to strip him naked and push him into a briar patch. What can I do?

Thank You So Much,
Heather Help Me

Dear Heather the Heathen,

It takes a heap a moldy stew to stump ole Crabigail, but I ain't rightly figgered out how to improve on the crunching sound of a naked man in a briar patch. Seems to me like he oughta crunch up purty good. So toss him on in there and get yerself some peace. Maybe some quiet-like Cream a Wheat.

Yers,
Crabigail

CR•ഇ

CHAPTER 18
SQUIRREL EGGS

I couldn't get a moment's peace from friends and family, including my own husband. Lord, he followed me everywhere I went, like he was Ruth and I was Naomi in the Bible. That whole whither I goest thing . . . I was watering the ferns on the front porch and turned to find him right behind me.

"Careful watering those ferns. I think there is a bird nesting in there."

"So what? Birds get rained on."

"Yes, but they don't experience tsunamis."

I brushed past him, and went to the kitchen to refill my pitcher. I carried it to the back porch to water the Snow White Waffle plant and Fluffy Ruffles. Dan followed right on my heels. He grabbed the broom and pretended to sweep, but I had done that earlier, and his task wasn't the least bit productive.

He said, "Watch Roxie and make sure it's not bringing squirrel eggs on the porch."

"I don't believe squirrels lay eggs. And, if they do, I've never seen our cat with one, but I'll keep an eye out for them. Maybe they'll taste good with bacon. And, quit calling her an *it*!"

"Well, squirrels have nests. You know what I mean."

"No, actually. I don't. Please, go play golf."

"No, I'm not leaving you alone."

"Look outside. There are TWO squad cars. Lizzie is upstairs, and Pam is here. I'm surrounded."

"I don't think it's enough."

"Dan, please. If you don't, I am going to have a nervous breakdown. I have stuff to do and you are in my way."

"I just can't. I'm worried about you. And worry will affect my chipping, so what's the point?"

"There are millions of sets of twins in the world. The odds of me being a victim are less than me winning a door prize at the

Kiwanis Christmas party. Thirty-three years, and I've never won one. And you bought that special chipping putter, so you'll be fine, too."

"It's a club, not a putter. A putter is a putter and a chipper is a wedge. In my bag is a wedge and also a sand wedge. In fact, I sometimes use a seven iron or an eight iron or even a nine depending on the loft I need. Some of the pros use a three wood to chip. Tiger Woods does that. But, there is no such thing as a chipping putter.

"Sort of like squirrel eggs?"

"If I go, do you promise to stay inside with doors locked?"

"Yes," I lied.

He called me between every single hole to see if I was okay. I swear I'm not going to survive this serial killer thing, and that doesn't even mean I'll get murdered. While he was gone, I sipped a glass of tea, and scrolled through Facebook. I even posted the squirrel egg story on my status and checked back frequently to see comments, haha's, and likes.

Andy Davis called me later. Andy was my very first employee when I was hired to coordinate arts for our town. In the early days, we ran the big art center by ourselves. He had seen my post on Facebook about Dan and the squirrel eggs.

"Hey, Andy."

"I just wanted you to know that I saw your post and squirrel eggs are very beneficial in nature. Although they are very rare, they are known for curing jock itch, hemorrhoids, hair loss, divorce, ear wax, sinusitis, mortgage payments, colon cramps, and Cream of Wheat. Good luck finding them!"

"Who knew there was a cure for Cream of Wheat or, for that matter, a need for one?"

"As I said, it is very rare."

My friends are both weird and funny.

"Andy, are you really calling to tell me to be careful?"

"Of course, I am. If a serial killer is murdering twins, he'll surely be looking for you and Pam."

"And why would that be, Andy?" I wasn't about to tell him about the message I'd received through Lizzie or about our upcoming trip.

"Trouble follows you. It just does. If I was a twin murderer, you and Pam would be top of my list."

"That's nice to know. Let's talk about your move to Dahlonega. You meet any nice ladies yet?"

We chatted for about twenty more minutes about his life and his new home. I tried my best to fix him up with Lizzie but that didn't fly. Still, it was great to take my mind off of fear and ugly things.

CR•ဆ

Dear Crabigail,

My wife constantly spills her sweet tea and coffee all over our brand new carpet and expects me to clean it up. Sigh! Can you help me?

Best Wishes,
Carrollton Carpet Cleaner

Dear Carpet Creep,

NO!!!! I got me enough to do answering dumb questions from dumber people than to come over to yore house and help you clean yore carpet. Besides, dirty carpet stains can save yore life. Some no account hoodlum breaks in yore house while you and the missus is sleeping. If he sees clean carpet, he's gonna think nobody lives there and come right on in. He could have a gun or a chainsaw, and y'all would be dead in less time than it takes to skin a possum. But if he sees fresh stains, he might skip y'all and murder yore neighbors instead. So next time yore wife sloshes her coffee or her properly brewed sweet tea you jest, smile and tell her thank you for keeping yore sorry butt alive.

Yers.
Crabigail

03•80

CHAPTER 19
PEOPLE WATCHING

Ryan called his dad from the airport. He was traveling ahead of Agent Candor to help coordinate the arrival of the twins traveling with other agents. They would be staying at a hotel set up as a safe house. The Feds acquired the whole building and had offices set up in some of the rooms. Agent Candor, himself, would arrive later in the day with a set of twins.

"Hey, Dad."

"You in Washington D.C.?"

"Not yet. I'm at the airport waiting on my flight. Just got through security."

"You doing good, Son. Your mom and I are proud. Working with the FBI . . . You're really making something of yourself."

"I have a good role model, Dad. And, this is temporary."

"Don't know about that. You catch that bad guy, Ryan. He done killed again I hear. And be careful. You be careful, Son."

"I will Dad. Love to Mom."

The young officer's night had been restless. He'd been wired up for the pending trip. When he finally dozed off in the wee morning hours, his demons returned to haunt him. He no longer dreamed of the scary movies of his youth. Now, his dreams were of dismembered corpses and bloody crime scenes. They always ended with a faceless blond man coming at him with a butcher knife. Ryan would wake, shaking in sweat, just before the blade pierced his chest.

Ryan sat quietly at the gate looking at the Coroner's Reports for the twentieth time, yawning, and periodically watching passengers come and go. He uncapped a yellow highlighter and covered an interesting sentence. Yellow highlights and pencil marks covered every page of the reports.

The sound of rolling wheels caused Ryan to look up. He saw a blond nice looking doctor stop by the gate agent's desk. Well, truthfully, he didn't know if the man was a doctor, but he looked like a professional of some kind. The man had a rolling carryon that looked like it could be a doctor's bag and it was long enough to hold a hack saw. It was square on the sides and black with a clasp on the front. On instinct, Ryan switched his phone app to photo and snapped a quick picture. He kept his eyes on the man.

A few minutes later, the blond man was joined by a dark-headed woman with two small children and a squirrely-looking teenager. The man and woman embraced, and he handed her the handle to the carryon. The man then retrieved an envelope from his coat pocket. From the envelope, he gave the woman a boarding pass. He also handed one to the teen boy. Looked like he held onto the passes for the little ones. The littlest of these, a girl, clung to her father's leg. They were just a normal family traveling to somewhere exciting.

Ryan shook his head and deleted the picture. Everyone was a suspect until they weren't. Everyone.

CR•ᘓ

Dear Crabigail,

Can you suggest a healthy diet to help me lose weight?

Sincerely,
Too Big For My Age

Dear Way Too Big and Getting Bigger,

Girls today expect some specialist like me to give em a quick and easy way to lose the flab they got watching soaps all day. They take them pills that make em pee all the time. They eat nuts, soybeans and raw vegetables till they get the constipation that just bloats em more. Then they want to cheat and git that laposuction. Well here's Crabigaille's laposuction: Suck in yer gut and git yer lap out from under that table. Quit eating squirrel food and get yoreself a well- balanced diet of fried chicken, fried okra, and fried potatoes.

Yers,
Crabigail

෬•෫

CHAPTER 20
KARMA

I finished packing my suitcase for the trip to D.C. I made sure to include my grey Allbird tennis shoes with new memory foam inserts. I would need them to push Pam around in her wheelchair. I expected we would do a lot of walking. Danger or not, I wasn't about to go to our nation's capital and not do some sightseeing. I knew Pam would agree.

I tugged my luggage down the hallway in search of my husband. A sign of things to come, the wheels went uncooperatively in opposite directions, and I found myself dragging the suitcase instead of rolling it. I found Dan in the living room hovering over the fish tank.

"Well, well. Look at you taking care of Judy. I can travel with the knowledge they won't starve to death."

All of my fish are named Judy. They're rescue goldfish. I named them all Judy to help restore karma after running over Pam's dog. I know that makes no sense to most people, but it was a dramatic and traumatic event in my life that I still struggle to recover from.

First of all, I didn't know that the bump I probably felt leaving Pam's driveway was her little beagle puppy, Judy. Pam didn't want to upset me at the time so she waited twenty-five years to tell me about it. The only reason she told me when she did is because it came up in conversation.

A few years back, Pam and I were chatting about her son Jarrett's new dog and that Jarrett had asked for name suggestions. I asked "How about Judy? Didn't you used to have a beagle named that? Whatever happened to Judy?"

Pam looked at me solemnly and said, "You killed her."

She went on to tell me that Judy had been asleep behind my tire in her ridiculously steep driveway and that she knew I hadn't realized I had done the awful deed. I was horrified.

"Oh Pam," I said. "I'm so sorry. I feel terrible."

"It was twenty-five years ago, so get over it."

Only I couldn't. It was as if I had killed the little lop-eared puppy just the day before. I had horrible dreams about it at night and dwelled on it all during the next few days. I kept picturing big teary puddle-filled dog eyes staring at me with great agonizing sadness. I would have preferred accusatory anger over the melancholy gaze that haunted me day and night.

A week later, I went to visit Mom in Blue Ridge. It was an annual visit I made every September to help her clean out the koi pond. The big orange and white fish had spawned and we scooped at least a hundred babies with a net and dropped them in a water-filled bucket. Mom normally took the babies to the local pond store and donated them to the owner. Unfortunately, I learned that the store had closed.

I asked Mom, "So what will you do with them now?"

"I know you'll think I'm awful, but I have no choice but to toss them in the woods. If I leave them in the pond they will overcrowd it, and I'll lose them all."

An hour later, I drove home with an old lidless cooler I'd found in the garage. I had it strapped in the passenger seat with the seatbelt. As I made the sharp curves on the mountain, the water would slosh to and fro and a fish or two would plop out and onto the floorboard where they would leap about in frantic disdain for oxygen. I would lean as far as I could without losing sight of the road, catch them with my right hand as I steered with the left, and put them back in the cooler. A few times, I had to pull over and retrieve one from under the gas pedal or the map pocket. It sure would have been handy if I'd found a cooler with a lid, but one has to make do when restoring karma.

As soon as I got home, I separated the fish into various containers so that they had room to stretch out and recover from their trip. I had bowls and buckets and coolers full of fish in the living room, dining room and kitchen. I named them all Judy and swore to them that I would find them good homes. And I did. I put notices out on all the social media I had at my disposal. I was very picky, and screened the adopters of the baby koi with due diligence.

I said "no" to a guy with big brass rings in his ears and what looked to me like self-made tattoos who wanted the whole lot. He said he would use them for snake food. I said "no" to a lovely lady with a blond ponytail and cowboy boots who wanted to put some of them in her horse trough to control algae.

I said "yes" to a group of seven girl scouts who came to the house with individual goldfish bowls. I made them promise to name the fish, "Judy." That was not negotiable, and they all solemnly agreed as they held three little fingers in the air. They left with fourteen free fish, and I purchased two boxes of trefoils and one box of thin mints.

Eventually, to Dan's relief, I found suitable homes for all the Judys except for five which I homed in my own aquarium. Four years later, they were all fat and happy and didn't seem to mind that they all had the same name. They shared their tank with a big black Plecostomus that I long ago named, Fred. Fred just sucked algae off the glass and the gravel and pretty much ignored the Judys.

I was happy to see Dan feeding Judy, and knew he would take good care of them while I was in D.C.

I asked, "Whatcha doing?"

"Feeding the Fish."

"I know that, but why are you crumbling up their fish pellets? Just drop them in as is."

"I do that, so that some will float down and that black guy on the bottom can have a chance."

"He's a Plecostomus. He doesn't need the pellets. He's an algae eater. Just drop the pellets in whole."

"That sounds to me a lot like one of those '*they say*' statements. How do you know he only eats algae?"

"My answer to that is the same answer that you give when Chris calls to tell us how tired he is after a grueling one hour performance on board his luxury cruise ship: "IT'S HIS JOB!"

"Hmmmph. I see you're packed. How long do you think this trip will last?"

"They said a week. You gonna miss me?

"I suppose. Goldfish aren't much company."

I kissed him right there with five little koi fish and one big, ugly Plecostomus looking right at me. Wonky-wheeled luggage, threatening serial killers, pushing my sister around in a wheelchair . . . none of that mattered. After all, I had karma.

CR•ဢ

Dear Crabigail,

My best friend told me a secret and made me promise not to tell anyone. I didn't think she meant I couldn't tell a couple of mutual girlfriends and now her secret is all over town. It's not my fault they blabbed it, but she won't speak to me. What should I do?

Thanks,
Besties No More

Dear Some Friend,

You ever heard a woodpecker pecking on a gutter in the spring? They do that cause it's mating season, and they try to be the loudest peckers, so the girl peckers will come a-flocking. What you need to do is find a great big iron stew pot. Know what a peckerhead is? It's someone with a hard head and a big mouth and yer the biggest peckerhead in town. So, I'd advise you to put that stew pot on yer head before you go out, unless you want one of them woodpeckers using yer peckerhead to find him a mate to tell all his secrets to.

Yers,
Crabigail

CHAPTER 21
BEFORE THE ARRIVALS

Ryan checked into the hotel via Federal employees who staffed the desk of the makeshift safe house. Agent Candor was still in Atlanta and would be coming later in the day with the Gardin twins.

After seeing to his room and luggage, Ryan went over the dossiers of all the twin pairs and waited in the lobby for each to arrive. It was a diverse, but friendly group all accompanied by seasoned FBI handlers.

Later, Ryan called Candy and chatted with her. She was on break at the Macon hospital where she worked as an emergency room x-ray tech. He couldn't give her a definite answer on when he would see her, and she understood. They both had crazy hours.

Ryan thought about calling his dad, but opted for a walk around the city instead. He had never been to the country's capital before. The early arriving twins were in their rooms, and he had some time on his hands.

He strolled up the steps of the powerful Jefferson Memorial taking in the view of East Potomac Park and the tidal basin. Just extraordinary. The structure was more impressive than pictures could possibly depict. Still, he dutifully snapped a good many to show his parents and girlfriend.

Ryan moved from portico to portico reading the words of wisdom inscribed from the writings of the nation's third President. He finished on the South side reading *"We hold these truths to be self-evident, that all men are created equal, that they are endowed by their Creator with certain inalienable rights, among these are life, liberty, and the pursuit of happiness . . ."*

He kept reading, but his mind was muddled by the great suffering of Ebodine and Stanley Washington and Carlson and Angela Armstrong. He had witnessed their anguish. Happiness.

Where was their happiness? Thomas Jefferson could make his grand guarantees, but even he couldn't rid the world from evil.

ℭ•ℬ

CHAPTER 22
FLYING'S FOR THE BIRDS

I shook Pam until she woke up.

"It's time."

"I'm not going."

"Yes, you are."

"Fine. I'll go, but we're driving."

"Nope. We are not driving all the way to D.C. It is time. You are fifty-three years old, and you are one of the bravest people I know. No, check that. You ARE the bravest person I know. You can get on that airplane."

"It's a Pringle can flying through the air. It's not natural. I'm not going."

"Don't be so dramatic! It is most certainly natural."

"God picked out who he wanted to fly: bugs and birds and whatever actress is playing Peter Pan on Broadway. Expendable things."

"So you think bald eagles are expendable? That's just un-American!"

"I didn't say anything about eagles."

"Special Agent Candor is going to accompany us."

There was a brief silence. Then a sigh. Not a resignation sigh, but a sigh of longing.

"Shemar."

I knew I had her. This time, I didn't tell her to quit calling him that.

"They are picking us up in an hour." I looked over at her open half-packed suitcase.

"What do I bring? Can I bring weapons? A parachute?"

"No. Just your clothes and toothbrush." I looked closely at her face. "And tweezers. Bring some tweezers. Somewhere, I have a *Helpful Tips on Flying* list. While you finish packing, I'll see if I can find it."

I couldn't resist having a little fun. Thirty minutes later she was packed and I handed her a sheet of paper, where I had hurriedly typed the following:

HELPFUL RULES FOR FLYING

1. To speed up boarding, lick the back of your ticket and stick it to your forehead.
2. Elastic is considered a hazard. All bras and panties must be carried through security in your hands.
3. Stop at the gate even if there is a line behind you. By rights as a first time flyer you get a set of wings to pin to your shirt. Let the folks in line know you can't proceed until you have your wings.
4. You also have a right to preflight alcohol. Demand a cocktail as soon as you board the plane. Tell them to make it a double.
5. Protect your overhead luggage storage by placing a sign in front of your carryon that says "This Space is Taken." People flying will understand that they cannot share your private compartment.
6. After boarding, recline your seat and pretend to sleep. By law, the flight attendants can't make you sit up if you are sleeping.
7. Demand to see the Pilot. Pilots are like rock stars. They love it when you ask for autographs..
8. There are rules about crossing over state lines in the air. Make sure you know each state's official song and sing it as we pass over.
9. To prevent air sickness give your onboard snack (usually 3 pretzels) to your sister.
10. If you hear the word "turbulence" that means that the plane is disintegrating and you should fall to the floor and scream, "We're all gonna die. We're all gonna die."

I know my sister better than anyone. A little humor would help settle her nerves, and make it easier for her to overcome her ridiculous fear of flying. It seemed to work. She laughed at every line of the list.

With Agent Candor seated up front with the driver and Pam and I in the backseat, we arrived at Hartsfield Jackson International Airport with little conversation. Pam looked a little green around the gills, but she wasn't backing out. I knew her fear was real when I noticed she wasn't drooling over the handsome FBI agent. She didn't call him "Shemar" once.

At the Atlanta airport, I was delighted with the preferential treatment we received. Agent Candor had prearranged for a wheelchair for Pam to be available as soon as we entered the terminal. It was bigger than Pam's and had mega wheels. We used Pam's personal wheelchair to transport our carryon luggage. Suitcases and Pam's walker were checked at the front entrance. We were escorted through and around the huge crowd waiting in line at Security by a lovely Delta employee. As we approached the Screening area, I told Pam to take off her shoes.

"Right," she smirked, but made no move to do as I said.

"Pam, seriously, take your shoes off."

She ignored me. We put our carryon items on the conveyor. The TSI agent, a large stern looking woman with no nonsense short grey hair said to Pam, "Ma'am I need you to take your shoes off and put them on the conveyor."

Pam put on her haughty face, but her shoes stayed put. "My sister put you up to that. I'm not falling for it or any of those things on her list."

"OMG, Pam," I said. "TAKE YOUR SHOES OFF." I looked at Agent Candor for help, but he was just laughing.

As a group, it took some doing, but we finally convinced her to take them off, and we sailed through security, the concourse train ride, and arrived at Terminal C without any more issues.

Finally, it was time to board the plane, and I could see Pam's face getting paler and paler. In contrast, there were red splotches breaking out on her neck and chest. I was worried she would back out, but she moved from her wheelchair to her seat by the window quietly. I sat next to her. Agent Candor was in the seat behind us. I saw him lean forward. He said encouraging, soothing words to Pam that should have made her swoon, but had little effect.

We sat on the tarmac for an eternity, which seemed to help settle Pam's nerves some. Time and boredom will do that. She even chatted a little. She discovered the Sky Mall Magazine and had a fit over a life-size Big Foot statue that she wanted to order for her front yard.

"You can take that magazine with you, Pam."

"Really? Cool. Oh, look at this. They have giraffe onesies. How cute! I have to get that for Rebecca for . . ."

The plane began to taxi.

Pam dropped the magazine and gripped my arm, her nails digging deeper than my cat Roxie, could ever manage. I dealt with it. If mauling me helped her through this then, fine, I could tolerate the pain, and the blood, and the scars that would probably follow.

As the plane gently, and with no bumpiness whatsoever, lifted off the runway in the most normal takeoff ever, Pam screamed "Shiiiiiiiiiiiiiiiiiiiiiiiiiiiiiiiiiiiiiiiiiiiiiiiiiiiiiiiiiiiiiiit." Her expletive lasted, pretty much, until the plane leveled out. All around us, people were laughing. They were sympathetic and amused and could tell it was my twin's first time flying.

When the light went off, the lovely flight attendant unbuckled from her jump seat and came to us.

"Are you okay, ma'am?" She asked with a smile.

Pam was calming down, but I answered for her.

"It's her first time flying. I think a cocktail might help her some."

"We'll be serving shortly, but maybe I could sneak her a drink now," she said with a wink. What would you like?"

Pam looked at her. "Heroin with a splash of cocaine."

I took over. "She would like a glass of Pino Grigio if you have it, and thank you."

The wine and time really did help, and Pam soon seemed to enjoy the flight. She kept her face plastered in the window looking out at the clouds, and as we descended, she could see the Washington D.C. landmarks. She pointed out the Pentagon, the Washington Monument and the Capitol building with amazement.

The flight attendant had obviously filled in the distinguished white-haired captain on their hilarious, first-time-flying passenger, because he was waiting for us as we de-boarded. He shook Pam's hand and asked, "How did I do flying my first plane?" Pam giggled at the joke. He then said, "Welcome to New York City." Pam brings out the comedian in everyone.

CR•SO

Dear Crabigail,

I have a pet peeve that I hope you can address. I can't stand when people expect me to use my phone as a phone. There is just no good reason for them to bother me with their out-loud rudeness. Just text me or Instagram me instead of calling me. Nobody likes to talk on the phone anymore. Don't you agree?

Signed,
Busy LA Girl.

Dear Too Busy to Call Yer Sweet Mama in LA Girl,

Well now, ain't that just a shame. You just go on with yer rude self and be too busy with yer tacky social life out in Californy or Lower Alabama, I ain't too sure which, to take a call from yer Sweet Mama. The Mama who done birthed you after twelve hours of hard, back breaking, sweaty labor with a do nothing husband who paid more attention to the hospital magazines than his wife's terrible suffering. The Mama who wiped yer dirty, smelly bottom and snotty nose and probably used two different rags to do that, and then had to wash em in her old rattling washer that her husband shoulda had fixed years ago or upgraded her to a new Sears model in harvest gold with a second rinse cycle with a complimentary dryer also in harvest gold that had a lint trap near the front that she didn't have to move the big bottle of Family Dollar bargain laundry detergent to get to it. The same Mama who drove yer butt to all them cheerleading practices, fixed yore sack lunches, and glittered yore science projects while you TALKED ON THE PHONE to yore good for nothing boyfriends.

So my answer to you is YES. Go ahead and Ignore yore sweet Mama and let her suffer in silence like she's done did all these years. She won't mind. Really, she won't.

Yers,
Crabigail

ᆑ•ᆒ

CHAPTER 23
PEEP HOLE

Cutie Pie Officer Ryan Jessup escorted us to our room on the eighth floor of the pretty hotel turned safe house, while Agent Candor took care of business we weren't privy to. Ryan even pushed the big brass rack that was piled up with our luggage. His room was right across the hall, and Agent Candor would be one floor down. I felt like I should tip the officer, but decided that might be insulting. I figured I would spring for a drink or something later, instead.

"Here you go, ladies. I'm right across the hall if you need me, and this card has my cell number and Agent Candor's, too. Don't hesitate to call us. Please do not leave this room for any reason without an escort. I'll even fetch ice for you before I settle in, and I'll be back at six to walk you to dinner."

He picked up our ice bucket and was out the door and gone before I could ask him . . . well it didn't matter. He would be back shortly. I was hoping the Coke machine would have decent bottled tea and wondered if it would be an imposition to ask him to walk me there. I would have to wait.

A minute or two later, I heard the tap tap at the door and opened it. I was delighted to see two bottles of Blue Leaf Sweet Ice Tea between Ryan's fingers and a full ice bucket tucked under his arm.

"You are the most thoughtful . . ."

"Ma'am, did you even look through the peep hole before you opened the door?"

Chagrined, I winced and shook my head.

"I want you to take the danger you are in seriously. You too, Ms. Pam."

"Oh, I would have looked if it had been me, and thank you so much for the tea."

After Ryan left, I took a look at our quarters. Pam claimed the bed near the window and was fluffing up her pillows against the padded headboard, so she could sit against them with her legs stretched out. She was educating herself on the remote control.

Our room was a suite with a pretty view of the D.C. Mall, two Queen-size beds, nice blue sofa and plush chair sitting area, big screen TV, and small kitchenette. As always I checked out the artwork envying the artist who had snagged such a lucrative contract. I wondered if this . . . I squinted . . . *C. Louise Gentry* . . . I wondered if she painted all of the paintings in every room of the hotel. What a coup that would have been for the artist.

Overall, the room was lovely except for . . . and, I didn't mean to be ungrateful, but really . . . the marble kitchenette counter boasted a measly two cup coffee pot. Beside it, sealed in plastic wrap packets were stir sticks, powdered creamer and hardened sugar. A stack of styrofoam cups sat nearby along with two tea bag-sized packets of coffee: one caffeinated, the other, Communist. There are more ways to kill me than chopping off my body parts.

Pam and I watched an episode of Dateline about a serial murderer, because we are both slightly demented that way. It was a good way to kill time . . . pun not intended . . . while we waited to be escorted to dinner. We freshened up, somewhat unpacked, and sipped glasses of tea. I wanted coffee, but wasn't sure how many miniature packets of grounds we would be allotted by the hotel. Until I knew for sure, I would wait for dinner. Thankfully, Officer Ryan knocked on our door, and I made sure he knew I peeped before answering as we proceeded to the hotel restaurant.

"It wasn't much of a peep," Pam said looking up at him as he rolled her to the elevator.

If I hadn't had such a caffeine withdrawal headache, I would have thought of a snippy comeback. I'd get even later.

Pam and I were a bit startled as we entered the private dining room. Already seated at the large mahogany table was Agent Candor and two sets of twin sisters.

"Welcome ladies. We'll make introductions shortly. Officer Ryan has one more set of twins to fetch first." Agent Candor nodded at Ryan and the policeman left to complete this task.

Pam and I pretended to look at the menu, but we were both looking around at the other twins. We weren't the only ones either.

The twins to our left appeared to be in their late twenties or early thirties. They were African American, short and pudgy, but lovely. The ladies both had braided, colorfully beaded hair that wound into interesting rivulets across the back and sides and beaded bangs that hung straight down on their foreheads. Thankfully, they were dressed differently, because otherwise, I absolutely could not tell them apart. Later in the evening, I noticed one put on thick-lensed glasses and thought that would help, until the other put on an equally thick pair. I knew instinctively that I would like these two.

The twins across the table were fascinating. You could see, if you looked closely, that the girls were born identical. Both were of average height, mid-forties, and when they spoke they sounded just alike. There was an exact symmetry to their facial features, but one was dyed blond with bouncy curls and a nice curvy figure. The other had longer, mousy-brown hair and a round, portly body that seemed odd on her five foot six frame. First thing I noticed was that this one was matronly plain-faced, wore no makeup and looked as if she hadn't seen a hairdresser in some time. Her sister, on the other hand, was very pretty. We could tell that she worked out, ate healthy, and took time to hone her appearance. Yet, they were identical biologically.

The dining room door opened and Officer Ryan ushered in two twenty-something statuesque redheads with four of what could not possibly have been real boobs hanging out of similar white low-cut tops. One wore a short red skirt that barely covered her panties . . . if she wore panties . . . and the other a pair of the tightest black capri leather pants I'd ever seen. That one most definitely did NOT wear underwear. They had on gobs of eye makeup, multi-pierced ears and thick red hair that curled around their shoulders. I had to grudgingly admit that they were gorgeous ladies despite their trashiness.

Pam whispered in my ear, "I have pantyhose looser than that."

I elbowed her as the redheads were seated to our right.

The FBI agent stood at the end of the table and introduced Pam and me first.

"To keep things simple, if you ladies all don't mind, we are going to refer to each set of twins by maiden names even if you are married. So Penny and Pam are the Gardin twins.

"Next we have Jakis and Jacqueline. They are the Ware twins."

I smiled at the two that I had already pegged as my favorite. I planned to ask them to braid Pam's hair before we flew home, even if my sister protested and I had to pin her down.

Nodding his head at the two ladies across the table, Agent Candor introduced them as Odene and Lureen Crosby. I smiled at them, too. The homely Odene smiled meekly back and the other spoke.

"Nice to meet all y'all."

Finally, he introduced the redheads as Savannah and Delanie Miller, and they greeted us all with gregarious hellos like they knew us all their lives. They chattered on about moving to Atlanta from Jacksonville, Florida, when they were teenagers and how they were both single, but always looking. I couldn't wait to hear Pam's opinion of them. Out of the assembled group, they were the only twins who had not born children, not that I was judging or anything.

Agent Candor encouraged us to order whatever we liked and to chat amongst ourselves and get to know one another.

"I'll explain what you are all here for in more detail after dinner."

I had to lean across Pam to chat with Savannah and Delanie.

"I love your red hair. Y'all live in Atlanta?"

Savanna said "We do. We share an apartment."

"What do y'all do in Atlanta?" I could only imagine.

Delanie grinned, "We're paid escorts."

Pam gave me a knowing look, raising one eyebrow like our Dad used to do. I know that my mouth dropped open, and I stammered out some kind of nonsense. I was thankful I didn't have tea in my mouth to spew across the table. Lureen giggled and Odene looked positively scandalized.

Savannah smacked her sister playfully on the shoulder.

"Ow! Don't hit me!" It was obvious they had played this game before.

Savannah portrayed a fake expression of exasperation. "Delanie loves to say that, because it's true. We own our own company. We and our employees actually escort wide loads down highways all over the country. We drive the guide vehicle."

Delanie handed out cards like any of us would be moving a house any time soon. I looked at mine. The company name on the card was DOUBLE TROUBLE ESCORTS. Yeah, no one would misinterpret that name.

"Oh!" Lurene Crosby said. "Like doublewides?"

"Yes Ma'am. Doublewides are big business for us."

"PAID ESCORTS!" Jakis laughed holding her glasses on to her nose by the bridge. "That is hilarious. If I was you I would NEVER explain it to folks. PAID ESCORTS! Oh Laws! Double Trouble Escorts! I bet y'all get all the business." Her laugh was infectious and soon we were all chuckling along with her.

Peach Cobbler and Coffee finished off a delicious chicken alfredo dinner for me and shrimp scampi for Pam. Agent Candor stood to start his presentation. Ryan remained seated. I wasn't sure how much he knew, or if he was kept in the dark like the rest of us.

"Ladies, you were asked to come here to our nation's capital under the protection of a joint task force composed of the FBI and the Atlanta Police Force. Each of you has received some kind of threat. Nods around the table acknowledged this to be correct. Because, you four, er eight have received specific threats, we brought you here to see if we can find a common element."

We were all paying close attention. Pam hung on the handsome agent's every word. I think I saw some drool drip on the dregs of her peach cobbler and roll into the melted ice cream. I rolled my eyes as Pam wiped her mouth with her napkin.

"Also, rest assured ladies that, as much as possible we are calling for local police forces and Sheriff's deputies to keep watch on the twins in their own communities. We think the target age is twenty to fifty, but that could change at any time."

Pam and I locked eyes. We both shared the same thought. Since we were a little more than fifty, maybe the serial killer would leave us alone. Doubtful though. After all, we had been contacted by him.

"Do any of you remember the missing and murdered children and young men of Atlanta back in the seventies?

Most raised their hands, though I know the redheads did not and seemed puzzled. Too young, I guessed.

"Lessons were learned from that era and the FBI has developed incredible investigatory resources. We can't protect everyone, but we can do our best to try. Officers from other states are being brought in to Georgia to help and volunteers are keeping an eye on twins in their hometowns. Hopefully, we'll catch this guy before he kills anyone else. Regardless, we are protecting possible victims as much as we can."

I think we all shared a sense of relief.

"During this week, we will have a variety of professionals interview you all, conduct tests, and glean whatever information might help. Some of you have special skills that we may tap into. Pam, for example, has a unique intuition that may prove to be helpful."

Pam sat up straighter and smiled adoringly. Lord, there would be no living with her now.

I know that the agent said a lot more, but my mind was beginning to wander, and I was quite frankly exhausted. Traveling had taken its toll on me. Thankfully, we were finally escorted back to our room.

I pushed Pam's wheelchair into the room and said goodnight to Officer Ryan. Pam stood and braced against the dresser to slip her jewelry off and find her pajamas. If she was half as tired as I was, she'd be in bed and asleep soon. I glanced over at the pathetic coffee pot and powdered cream packets, dreading the morning. I missed my own appliances; I missed my meandering half and half; and I missed Dan.

CR•ᵹ

Dear Crabigail,

I really need your help. I married a man whose first wife died some time ago. It seems he wanted to stay close to her so he mixed her cremains in a can of paint and painted the walls with it. I have to live in this house and it gives me the creeps. Can I wallpaper over his wife?

Yours,
New Wife in Nebraska

Dear Tarnished Trophy Wife,

Cause I done had me a double buttered Velveeta grilled cheese for lunch, and I'm in a particular good mood, I'm gonna give ya two possible answers, and you can pick which one you want. Don't matter much to me.

Firstly, Get ya some of that Crime Scene Spray that they use on that show CSI. Shemar is on that show, ya know. Anyways, spray them walls good. Then when he goes to bed, plug in a black light. When he gets a gander at them glowing walls I betcha he'll be stoked up his own self to wallpaper over that dead wife.

Now, if ya don't like that one, and you got a mind to, then ya could try this: Them ashes has bits of bones and teeth in em, don't they? Folks around these parts pay good money for texturing. So, wait til he kicks the bucket and do the other walls to match up.

I mighta come up with a third one if I had the time or keered to, but if I dilly dally anymore I'll miss my soaps, and my other double buttered Velveeta grilled cheese'll get itself burnt.

Yers,
Crabigail

CR•ЯO

CHAPTER 24
BUTTERED TOAST AND OATMEAL

We filled our plates from the complimentary breakfast provided by the hotel. I'm not sure why, but when I travel I always go for a steaming bowl of oatmeal with a sprinkle of brown sugar and cream, and buttered toast. Except for the toast, I never eat that at home. I scooped up scrambled eggs, a blueberry-toasted bagel with cream cheese, and crisp as a ladder, bacon for Pam.

We settled into the large booth with the other ladies and joined in the pleasant morning chatter. The coffee was heavenly, and the pretty waitress made sure my cup stayed full.

Lurene told Pam that she was a fan of her Crabigail series. She had a lot of questions for my sister.

"Where on earth do you get your ideas?"

Pam smiled. "I don't know where they come from."

"I can tell you," I said. "She has a wicked mind. Always has."

Pam ignored me. "I draw a lot from my childhood, especially conversations with my dad."

Delanie leaned forward. Her tight, emerald green blouse dipped low beneath her bosom. I was impressed that she could breathe. "Was your father anything like Crabigail? Savannah and I read your column every day, too." Savannah, with a mouthful of pancake nodded in agreement. I couldn't help but notice that syrup dripped into her cleavage. I looked up at the ceiling, pretending to admire the white suspended tiles.

"Well, no; not exactly, but sometimes his wisdom was hilariously off-kilter." Pam paused, tilting her head to the left, and I could tell she was in her weird thinking mode. "Here's an example that, when the time is right, I'll work into a *Dear Crabigail* answer. When I was a teenager, I had just been dumped by a boy right before Prom. I complained to my dad that, if I missed Prom, it would be the worst day of my life. He gave me this advice: 'Go outside and catch yourself the ugliest, slimiest toad frog you can find. Then swallow it. Nothing that happens to you after that will be worse, and you will have used up your worst day ever.'"

As our new friends laughed, Pam added, "I think I inherited that kind of brain."

I nodded. "I can vouch for that!"

While we ate, we compared notes on the horrific messages that had brought us all here. The Ware twins had both received a text message that read, *I'm coming for you 2 blackbirds next. Plucking you right outa your nest.* The Miller girls had received a message on their company email: *A pair of boobs will complete my collection. And when I say a pair, I mean 4. Got just the knife.* Odene's message had come just to her: *Where is your sister? The pretty one? Maybe I'll give you some of her pretty parts when I cut you both up. Twins share don't they:* A sick mind wrote those messages, regardless of whether he was the actual murderer.

Ryan gave us a rundown of the day's activities. It seemed we would all be working with a team of psychologists and psychiatrists who would examine our brains to find out if we had anything in common amongst ourselves, or to the dead victims. There was also some attention to the psychic connections we may or may not share.

I would have guessed that of all the twins present, the mismatched Odene and Lurene would be the most unlikely to share psychic abilities. I was wrong. Their connection was oddly very strong. Testing involved matching cards, and sketching pictures transmitted through the air by our twin partners. I failed miserably, while Pam scored higher than anyone else. The Ware twins did about the same as I did, while the red-haired Miller twins were somewhere in the middle.

After lunch, we filled out pages and pages of questionnaires. They asked about our education, favorite foods, trips we'd taken, past relationships, hobbies, and our sex lives. We had to list every person we had ever known. Leaving no stone unturned, my brain was about fried. I needed coffee.

Afterwards, I waited in the lobby with an officer I didn't know while they continued questioning Pam. They all seemed fascinated by her abilities, and I could see why. My sister is a mysterious soul with strange gifts that often freak me out and get me in trouble. Sometimes though . . . rarely really . . . I'm sort of grateful for her crazy brain. People who don't believe in mind reading haven't met Pam. I hoped she could use those gifts to catch the scary, evil man. At the same time, I hoped she wouldn't use her gifts in a way that got us killed.

CR•ᏚᎧ

Dear Crabigail,

The last of my eight children just left for college, and I miss them all so much. I don't know how my husband and I will handle this quiet house. Any suggestions?

Sincerely,
Esther

Dear Empty Nester Esther,

You got bigger problems than you know. Now that all them kids is gone, yer hubby is gonna want to do the dirty all day long, seven days in a row. He'll be wanting it right on the kitchen table even before you git the supper dishes cleared. He'll want it on the recliner during Days Of Our Lives, right during the good parts, even when Marlena is about to be rescued from Stefano's dungeon by John, who's gone blind and can't remember stuff. What you need is a hobby. I'd suggest taking up sewing. Then every morning, while he's asleep, sew up the seams of his boxer shorts a little. He'll think he's gittin fatter and start going to the gym. Plus, when he's acting friskier than a pup with an old shoe, it'll take him a while to pull off his boxers giving you time to make yer git away.

Yers,
Crabigail

ରେ•ଛ

CHAPTER 25
DADDY

Sierra looked across the room at her sister. She had no choice really. The paralysis included her eyes. Cheyenne looked right back at her, back-lit by the picture window, tied to a chair, unblinking.

Their daddy, Joe loved his pickup trucks and so, when the twins were born, he insisted on naming them after his two favorites. Thankfully, their mom shared his sense of humor and went along with the names. Four years before, on their sixteenth birthday Joe gave her a brand new Cheyenne truck, and he gave Cheyenne a brand-spankin' new Sierra. He said it was just two weird to give them their namesake vehicles. The girls thought it was hilarious, and hugged their father's neck, before taking them for a spin.

There had been pressure on her bladder before. Now, it was gone. She must have peed herself, but she couldn't feel it.

A year after the girls received their pickups, Joe would be dead. A fall from scaffolding on a high-rise building, on which he was construction foreman, plunged him twenty-seven stories to a Peachtree Street sidewalk. Their mom chose cremation. There just wasn't enough left of their daddy to bury proper.

Their mom, Celeste, sunk into a depression that came and went. The girls looked in on her when they could. Celeste didn't have many friends. She lived off the settlement she received, and spent most of her days in front of the television. Sierra wasn't sure their mom even noticed when the twins moved out and into their own apartment. They took Joe's urn with them. The sight of it made their mother cry. The girls kept Celeste's refrigerator filled and made sure her bills were paid, but the happiness of their childhoods was a distant memory.

Sierra's mouth was so dry; so very dry. Why couldn't she move? Or swallow? Or breathe? She could smell, though. It was the scent of the sandalwood candle she had lit . . . was it just an hour ago? Candles always relaxed her . . . the irony of that. She would have laughed had she been able.

She couldn't see Cheyenne now. Something was blocking her. Someone. A person . . . now stepping to the side . . . holding something. It was her father's urn, and it was open. She heard the lid shatter to the floor. It startled her, but she couldn't jump despite the fright of it.

She could see Cheyenne again. Grey powder crumbled from her open mouth. Fascinating. Horrific. She watched as the light faded from her sister's eyes.

The killer turned and walked slowly to Sierra . . . closer now . . . peering into her still eyes . . . holding up the urn . . . and a wooden spoon. Sierra wished desperately to scream, but she couldn't. Her mouth hung open, though. She could tell. Her mouth was dry. Her tongue hardened. Water . . . she needed water badly.

It was all hopeless. Sierra could only look into her killer's cold dark eyes as her own light faded, and her father's ashes were spooned into her frozen open mouth.

CR•ЄD

CHAPTER 26
SINYLCHOLINE SUCKS

Agent Candor addressed us before lunch. "Ladies I know this isn't the best dining conversation, but I need to inform you that there has been another twin murder in Atlanta. Sierra and Cheyenne Handley, age twenty, were found dead in their shared apartment, despite Police presence in the area. Unfortunately, we just don't have enough manpower to protect everyone, but we are doing the best that we can. The Governor has reached out to other states for additional assistance, and I'm sure he will receive compliance. In the meantime, we will remain vigilant providing protection for the eight of you."

"Oh, no." I was horrified.

Jakis raised her hand. "Agent Candor. Did they have body parts chopped off like the other girls?"

"I'm sorry, ma'am, I can't really talk about those details. I can tell you, however, they were injected with Succinylcholine, a paralyzing drug used in surgical settings. They basically suffocated as their ability to breathe shut down. Succinylcholine is very difficult to detect, and we got lucky. I'm releasing that information to you, because we believe the perp has medical training. There is consideration in the department that you ladies, those of you with some intuitive abilities, might be able to provide valuable insight that could help the investigation. Frankly, I'm a little skeptical about that, but I'm willing to explore all options.

"Lord, does this man ever talk like he's not on Hill Street Blues?"

Pam nudged me with her elbow despite the fact that I was whispering.

I wrote the name of the drug on my legal pad "sucksenalcholine" so I could Google it later. Google would correct my spelling with it's *Did You Mean* feature.

"Furthermore, the Coroners in the other cases have now confirmed that the same drug was used in the other murders. They just didn't know to look for it before. It's very hard to find unless you deliberately test for it. We will release more information when we can."

He looked up from his documents.

"We have agents in Atlanta investigating. The girls' mother, Mrs. Handley is, of course, devastated. The family has her hospitalized and sedated. For now, I think the FBI will stand down from interviewing her."

My thoughts went to the mother. Poor thing. I couldn't begin to put myself in her place . . . what I'd do if it were my children.

Jakis wasn't through. "So, how about those other girls? Is there more stuff about them that we don't know?"

Her sister chimed in. "We watch all the crime shows. Sometimes you people hold back so's the perp can confess, and he'll know all about the murder. So when he confesses, he'll say facts only the murderer will know. Ain't that right?"

You could tell this had been a subject of much discussion between the two of them, and we all found it interesting. We wanted to know, too.

Agent Candor smiled at the Ware sisters. "You ladies are absolutely correct." And with that, he walked out of the room.

"Well! That was no help a'tall." Jakis was miffed. Jacqueline just shrugged, and took a bite of her chicken salad sandwich.

I didn't feel much like eating, and asked for coffee, instead. The cute little waitress brought me a Styrofoam container for my sandwich and chips, along with a paper cup, wrapped in a cardboard sleeve, filled with coffee. As I loaded my sandwich into the container, Pam reached over and snagged my pickle. Murder and mayhem don't ruin her appetite. I gave her my most sarcastic look.

"Help yourself, why don't you?"

"Sorry. I couldn't help it. You know I don't even like pickles, but my mouth tastes like ashes."

"Hamburger over cooked?" I didn't wait for her answer, as everyone was getting up from the table. I pushed Pam's wheelchair to the elevator, managing my cup and the chair handle with practiced dexterity. My Styrofoam container rode in Pam's lap.

Later, we all gathered in the Ware twins' room. We sat on their beds and chairs, and watched the news. Pam was feeling pretty good, and had managed the short trip down the hall with her walker. The newest murders were on every channel. We all wanted to know what happened to those girls with the Western sounding names. We also felt the need to be together.

Pam looked over at me. "Pickup trucks."

"Huh?"

"You're thinking about Westerns, about old Western movies, but they were named after pickup trucks."

I knew instinctively that she was right. I admit, not for the first time, I was a bit jealous at her mind reading, plus a little creeped out. I would give anything to know how she does that.

CR•ꙅᗞ

Dear Crabigail,

So, I've got a problem with a staircase I want to build up to our second floor attic that I'm trying to convert to usable space. The ceilings are ten feet, seven and three quarter inches and the distance to the foyer (I don't want the step to extend past the gables there) is about twenty feet less about five eights of an inch. I'm using solid knotted oak with spindles, and I'd like to have a landing on the fourth step up. I know you're supposed to take the total height between floors in inches and divide by 8.5, but the landing's got me off somehow. Can you tell me the dimensions I should use for the risers?

Sincerely,
Do it Myself, Dad

Dear, Don't Do it Dad,

No.

Yers,
Crabigail

CR•ဢ

CHAPTER 27
THE FEELS

The Ware girls' room was probably the same size as the rest of the suites, but the square layout made it seem roomier. Our room across the hall was long and narrow. We left ours in kind of a mess. Pam's suitcase was open on the floor with clothing spilled out. I put most of my things in the closet, but my usual assortment of cosmetics were strewn over the bathroom counter. We had a nice selection of snacks scattered on the dresser and microwave, with a gallon of tea iced down in the sink. The tea wouldn't fit in the mini-fridge.

I had to admire the housekeeping skills of Jakis and Jacqueline. Those two had already transferred their clothing to the chest of drawers, stowed their luggage in the closet, and didn't have the clutter piled up like we did. I made a mental note to straighten up our mess, even though I knew I would do no such thing. The Ware's room soon became the natural and most comfortable group hangout.

It's hard to explain to singles about the bond twins feel . . . and not just with their own twin . . . but also the kindred connection to other pairs. We have no trouble telling identical twins apart, either. The Crosby girls, Odene and Lurene were identical, but time and attention made them look fraternal. The Ware and Miller girls were probably identical. I say probably, because I think the FBI folks assumed that my sister and I were, but we are in fact fraternal. We just look and sound alike. That does not mean we are identical, as we didn't share a placenta in our mother's womb.

I sat in the armchair with my feet on the ottoman. Pam was next to me in her wheelchair. Delanie sat on the bed closest to the door with her back against the quilted headboard. Jakis lay on her belly, in front of her, at the foot of the bed. Jacqueline sat cross-legged on the other bed, with Odene and Lureen beside her.

Odene lay back on her elbows. Savannah sprawled on the red sofa, hugging a cushion. Every once in a while, we could hear a cough or a muffled radio conversation from the FBI agent outside the door.

Most of our chatter was about the psychic testing, and who did or didn't have mad sixth-sense skills. Most of us didn't or couldn't access those skills, just Pam and the Crosby twins. We drilled all three of them with questions.

I asked Lurene and Odene which one had the strongest abilities.

They looked at each other, communicating in that silent twin way that Pam and I have done our whole lives. I don't think of that as a special skill, though. It's just something that comes natural to twins.

Lurene spoke. "We're about equal, I guess. It used to be just between us, you know. We'd know somehow what each other was thinking or feeling, but over time that changed, didn't it, Odene?"

Odene nodded. "Somewhat."

Lurene continued. "Over time, that changed up a bit. We began to get the feels . . . that's what we call it . . . the feels . . . what other people was feeling."

"Once, we helped a girl's family find her that'd gone missing. Too bad she was dead."

Odene chimed in. "She was drowned in the river. Her daddy did it. We told the police. Took em. . . ."

Lurene took over. ". . . only a week to find her. We told em where to look, though."

". . . and who did it."

CR•SO

Dear Crabigail,

I'm going on a cruise with my grandchildren. They are worried about my swimsuit choice. How old should a woman be before she stops wearing a bikini?

All the Best,
Yellow Polka Dotty

Dear, Hotty Dotty.

I went to the beach last year and was horror fried at what some of them gals was wearing. Some of em didn't have on much more than two bandaids and a cork. Anyways, I spread out my towel and stretched out for a nap, but these bratty kids kept running around, hollering and kicking sand. They kept up the ruckus, and I told em to shush up. They started making fun of my red striped one piece, calling it a granny suit, so I took it off and flung it at em. Far as I'm concerned, you can quit wearing yer bikini anytime you want. Just maybe, don't quit wearing it at the Water Park, or they'll take back yer season pass.

Yers,
Crabigail

⌉•⌊

CHAPTER 28
ROBBIE

The next day, we were split up. Pam and I were taken to the basement at a Federal building to the office of the record keeper, Robbie Perkins. Agent Candor wasn't with us. Another agent, Tony, escorted us. Tony told us all about Robbie on the walk over. Robbie had been a ladder climber at the FBI on his way to becoming a Field Agent and one day, possible Director, when a female suspect in a child kidnapping case upended his career by shooting him in the back.

The woman, Vesta Lee, had ambushed Robbie outside a seedy motel when a tip had led him there. The suspect, a survivalist, had burgled the baby boy from his crib in the middle of the night. She had help, of course. Her boyfriend, Amos Cottrell, was a long time drug addict who would do anything Vesta Lee wanted. He had climbed through the bushes, duct taped the window of the nursery, and then tapped the glass out with a hammer. Amos used his dirty t-shirt to protect Vesta Lee from glass shards, and hoisted her through the window. He winced a little at the shrubbery scratches on his bare chest and arms, but made sure she made it in and out unscathed. Due to Vesta Lee's practiced stealth, and the tape muffling the sound of glass breaking, the parents had slept right through it.

Now, Amos was inside the motel yelling at the baby to shut up. Amos had seven outstanding warrants for assault and drug possession. He was wanted in three states. Robbie assumed Vesta Lee was in there, too. He wanted badly to bust the door in.

Robbie could hear Amos yelling louder through the thin walls. A TV blared "Let's Make a Deal." He knew other agents and local police were on their way to help, and could hear the sirens a few miles away. Unless, he detected Amos' anger escalating to harm the child, he would wait for the backup.

Only the FBI knew who the subjects were, and managed to successfully keep it from the media. The press spun the same lack of news with repetitive footage of the crying parents. When that grew old, there was some media speculation that the baby may have been taken by a desperate childless couple. Other sources claimed the parents killed the baby and hid the body. Robbie knew better. Vesta Lee and Amos planned to sell the little boy on the adoption black market. White babies bring a lot of Meth money.

Robbie could hear the infant crying inside. He had his gun drawn with left shoulder on the door frame, when Vesta Lee came from behind and fired. As Robbie fell, he spun and shot the woman in the forehead. Amos heard the gunshot and cracked opened the door with his own gun drawn. All Amos saw was Vesta Lee. It took a few seconds to understand the red cubes around her. She'd gone for ice, and dropped the bucket as she fell. The ice cubes were coated in the spurting blood. Distracted, Amos didn't look down at his feet where Robbie lay. Robbie shot up and blew a hole through Amos' chin and out the top of his head.

Before backup arrived, Robbie dragged his paralyzed body into the room where he found the infant on a pallet on the floor. He held the baby in his arms above the pool of blood that oozed from his own injury, and cooed softly. It took some doing to get him to let go of the child, and allow the EMTs to save his life.

Robbie overcame the doctors' predictions that he would never walk, but the debilitating injury ended any chance for further advancement. He was only thirty-eight when it happened. Once he was able, he found work at the records desk. Not the career move he expected.

The agency considered Robbie to be a hero and a National treasure. He would have a job and a purpose as long as he wanted.

Pam and I were introduced to Robbie. Though we'd heard his story, we were taken aback by his appearance.

Robbie had the tiniest, skinniest body I've ever seen on an old man to sport such a huge and odd drooping belly. He walked hunched over with tiny little shuffling steps, which made his belly swing to and fro, bouncing off his knees. You couldn't help but stare.

Back in the day, before the shooting, Robbie was purported to be quite the lady's man. I imagined if you stretched him up to his thirtieth birthday height he might be at least five foot ten. As he stood now, at age seventy, he barely reached five feet. In his prime, back when he was somebody, Robbie was a handsome man, and enjoyed many girlfriends, and a succession of wives, sometimes at the same time. Now he was seventy and lived alone . . . no wife, no children, no siblings, no dog. He refused to retire, and the powers that be didn't have the heart to force him.

We sat at a table and looked at images of men, suspects in other crimes. These were suspects that had photos attached to their files, but no DNA. We didn't have a clue what we were supposed to look for. Robbie seemed to understand that.

"Just look at 'em and if anything . . . calls out to you . . . let me know. Even if it's just a feeling."

We stayed there for hours until Ryan came and walked us back to the hotel. We had looked at hundreds of pictures. No feelings. No aha moments. But, we were doing our part and that mattered.

CR•ƧⱭ

Dear Crabigail,

My son is 26 years old and won't help around the house. He's a slob. How do I get him off the pot and motivated?

From,
Fed Up in Franklin

Dear, Maybe You Done Fed Him Too Much,

If yer son ain't pulling the plow around the house, ain't nobody's fault but yores. You went and raised him womper-jawed. Ain't too late to straighten him out, tho. There's always some woman around needing a man to keer for. So, look around town. Check the beauty pageants where the purty ones hang out. Rustle him up a wife, and let him go pee all over her pot.

Yers,
Crabigail

ᴄ⳿•⳿ᴅ

CHAPTER 29

MOM CALLS . . . AGAIN

I opened my left eye and groaned. Pam's phone was ringing . . . or singing rather. Queen's *Somebody to Love,* was blasting away, and I knew it was Mom calling. She's a big Freddy Mercury fan, and Pam made Mom's favorite song her ringtone. Pam had different ringtones for just about everyone. Even the garbage man had one. His was *Take Out the Trash* by some group called They Might Be Giants. Mine used to be Train's "Hey Soul Sister," but Pam found some, unheard of before, annoying *Sister, Sister* song to replace it. Still I couldn't complain. The year before, she designated my ringtone as *The Bitch is Back,* by Elton John. Mom fussed at her for that one, and made her change it.

Pam was sleeping right through Freddy, so I grappled across the little table between our beds and found her phone.

"Hi, Mom! What time is it?"

"It's seven. Now, before you fuss, I was calling Pam, but somehow I called you instead. I don't understand why my smartphone does stuff like this. It can't seem to tell you two apart."

Mom and I have made a truce of sorts. She won't call me before eight anymore, and in exchange, I won't spend five minutes of her life complaining about how early it was.

"Mom, your phone is not trying to trick you. You DID call Pam. She's asleep, so I'm answering her phone to keep from waking up everyone in the hotel."

"Well since you're awake, I guess I'll just talk to you. You girls helping the police find the murderer?"

"We are. Should have it wrapped up by lunch." I'm snarky when I get woken up and haven't had coffee. Can't help it.

Mom knew I was being sarcastic and chose not to address it, but I could tell she was a little annoyed with me. "I just saw on the news where he murdered some more twins. Well, that's all I wanted to say. You can go back to sleep now. Bye."

Like I could go back to sleep with that news. I got up and made a tiny cup of coffee in my tiny hotel-supplied coffee pot, and sipped it quietly. I had my back to Pam, with my feet up in the window sill, watching the sun peek up. Me and the sun and the clouds. Not real clouds, just clots of powdered cream floating in my coffee. I was pretty sure Mom and I were the only two up at this ungodly hour. I would watch the news later and find out more about the murders, but right then, I just needed to meditate peacefully.

Pam stirred around 7:30, and we both showered and dressed for the activity packed day. Pam and the Crosby twins had more ESP sessions with a slew of Psychiatrists. The other girls would go over pictures of Atlanta medical personnel. I didn't have Pam's abilities, but I guess the investigators thought more of the no DNA criminal files might trigger something. Honestly, I think they just didn't have anything else for me to do.

Cutie Pie Ryan escorted me to Robbie's office around nine. This time, Robbie had a new project for me. I was to look at twin murder cases from way back. I was soon lost amid dusty old files going back thirty years or so. I made dutiful notes on a legal pad supplied by Ryan with case numbers and details that I thought might be relevant.

Few of the cases involved the actual murder of a set of adult twins. There was one case where a jealous husband shot his wife and her twin sister, who just happened to be there at the time. And, there were several where young moms killed their twin infants at birth through drowning or smothering. Very sad.

The old files did include murders of one twin, and sometimes, it was one twin killing the other. I've been tempted to do that myself a few times. One attempted murder was a doctor, pregnant with twins, who hammered a nail into her husband's forehead. Somehow, he survived. What the heck? Totally, not the same thing, but I wrote the details down anyway.

I'm a writer. Maybe my notes would come in handy someday for a book or a short story.

Ryan was across the room digging out boxes. Robbie kept me company at the table and we progressed, from discussing the files, to talking about the current murderer and his victims.

"Robbie, do you have any thoughts on why this guy does what he does? It's so evil."

He nodded. "I have some thoughts on it, but I'm not supposed to influence you ladies."

I looked at him with my eyebrows raised. Pretty sure, if I could see a mirror, I would look just like my dad. Pam and I inherited his animated eyebrows.

Robbie looked around to reassure himself that Ryan was out of ear-shot. He leaned forward and whispered, "Pay close attention to the family interviews on the TV. There's something there. You might learn something from 'em. Listen to the moms. They suffer."

I started to ask him what he meant, but Ryan came over to the table, and ushered me out to return to the hotel and lunch.

We had lovely chicken crepes and pear salads. The wait staff kindly brewed a pitcher of sweet tea for all of us Georgia girls. We didn't say anything about the lemons on our glasses, but every one of us quietly removed the offensive fruit. Except for Pam, that is. She loves lemon in her tea, or worse, lime. The thought of citrus tainting my tea makes me cringe. I don't understand how we're even related.

As usual, Agent Candor spoke during lunch and told us about another set of twins, murdered the night before. Agent Candor never seemed to mind that his daily talks were absolute appetite killers for some of us; never Pam, though. I think Aliens dropped her off while Mom was having me. Back then, they anesthetized the moms, so it's not like she would have known.

Agent Candor showed us pictures of the newest victims, beautiful blondes with . . . had to be contact produced . . .

gorgeous emerald green eyes. Their names were Summer Treasure Hunt and Autumn Fox Hunt. My first thought was they must have delightful parents to name them such fun names, but I was wrong. Their father died of a heroin overdose several years before, and their mom had drug issues of her own. According to the Agent, Mom had a rap sheet five pages long from various narcotic arrests. The twins raised themselves, worked hard at minimum wage jobs, and put themselves through college. Summer and Autumn were determined to make a better life for themselves, and now they were dead. What a shame.

Only, it was worse. We learned that the murderer removed, and took with him, those beautiful eyes. This man was a monster. The FBI had their reasons for wanting us to know that, I guess.

I shook my head to clear my thoughts so that I could focus on what Agent Candor was saying. He'd mentioned the DNA again, and I wanted to pay attention. I'd hoped for something like this.

"We were able to isolate semen on both of the girls. The DNA matches semen found on some of the other victims. Not all, but some."

Lurene spoke first. "That's fantastic. Sickening, but fantastic."

Jakis raised her hand. "Can you tell anything new from the DNA?"

The Agent nodded. "Actually, we can tell a lot."

I flipped to a clean page in my legal pad and took notes. "Can you tell us more about who he is, and why he's terrorizing twins?"

Jaqueline was fascinated, too. "Lordy, please don't be a black dude."

Jakis asked, "So they've all been raped? If y'all got sperm, then they've been raped, right?"

Agent Candor directed his response to the Ware twins. "Not necessarily. There is no evidence of rape of any of the victims. It's more likely that he ejaculated after each murder. Some killers, especially serial killers, get a sexual thrill from the acts, the killings.

Preliminary tests tell us a lot. We know that this man is Caucasian and most likely has blond hair. It narrows the pool significantly, but we're still talking about millions of suspects out there."

"Okay, that's good." Jacqueline was relieved.

"Laws," said Delanie. "Who would have thought you'd get hair color from a drip drop of sperm."

"Yuck." That was Savannah's whole contribution to the conversation.

I felt a chill. Evidence was coming together. A sense of excitement was building in the room, and chatter continued to roll.

Jacqueline blurted out, "I knew it was a white man. Had to be."

But then I looked at Pam and saw her forehead furrowed and the slow shake of her head. "Uh Oh." I know that look and what it meant. Still, I was perplexed. "What?" I had to ask her.

"Something's not right," she said. "I'm confused. This isn't right at all."

Agent Candor looked befuddled. He leaned over the table studying Pam's face. She just kept shaking her head back and forth.

Odene, who hardly ever spoke up, said quietly, "I feel it too Pam. Something's wrong."

"What are y'all talking about?" I admit that I didn't understand them at all. I looked at Lurene. "How about you?" I looked back at Pam, "And, wrong about what?"

Lureen was sitting beside my sister and nodding her head. It was such an odd partner to Pam's head shaking back and forth. I resisted the urge to nod and shake my head in sequence. So, I rocked in my chair, instead. These two had me so confused. Agent Candor waited patiently.

"It's a woman," Pam said softly.

Agent Candor tilted his head and studied her face. His tone matched hers. "DNA says different."

"DNA is wrong."

Ryan was as confused as the rest of us. "DNA can't be wrong. It's . . . It's Science."

Pam looked over at him. "I know it is, but I'm telling you. The murderer is a woman. I don't know how, and I can't explain the semen, but I know it's true, and I know I'm right."

Odene was still nodding. So, she agreed with Pam. I couldn't for the life of me figure out how that could be, but I knew that Pam was hardly ever wrong. I'd trust her weirdness over science any day.

We all returned to our rooms for a break, and I'm sure the other twins were doing the same thing Pam and I were doing. We had the TV on CNN watching the news coverage of the murders of Treasure Summer Hunt and her sister Autumn. The reporter found the girls' mom, Ashley, and was trying her best to interview the strung out woman. It was a pathetic sight. The woman was nervous and jittery and kept scratching at her arms. She had dirty blond stringy hair that hung over her face. She was wearing a tank top and shorts, which accentuated her skeletonized skinny body. Scars and bruises were visible all over her arms and face. Thank you HD TV.

"Ma'am . . . Ashley . . . Can you tell us about your daughters?"

"They's my girls. They's always been my girls. What am I gonna doooo?" The word "do" transitioned into a loud wail. "They's all chopped up. He took their eyes. Their beautiful eyes!" Agent Candor told us this information, earlier. Apparently, he knew we would see this interview on the news. Some things, even the FBI can't keep quiet.

The reporter had her "I'm so concerned" professional expression going. "Ma'am, when did you last see your daughters?

More wailing.

She reminded me of that lady that was going to Bingo. What was her name? Ebodine. She'd had parts of her girls tied to her car. The news never interviewed her; couldn't, but they had video of her coming home from the police station wailing something awful.

"Do you have any idea who could have done this?" The reporter was relentless.

More wailing. More scratching. It was so sad.

I jumped up from the bed, and grabbed Pam's leg. I remembered what Robbie said. I thought about all of the other interviews of the murdered twin's mothers we had sadly watched over the last weeks, and I had an intuition of my own.

"Ow! Let go of me!"

"Pam! He. . . SHE if it's a she . . . is not punishing the twins at all. She's punishing their mothers!"

CR•ℛ

Dear Crabigail,

I am in quarantine with my two cats, cause the doctors says I'm contagious with the flu. I haven't seen another human being in two weeks. Are you still out there? If you are, whatcha doing?

Signed,
Bored Barbara Going Bonkers in Bremen

Dear Barbara the Crazy Cat Lady,

My sister Erleen's one of them crazy cat ladies, too. Yer problem is you ain't got near enough cats, so you's jest borderline crazy. Ring on down to the shelter and see if you can get yoreself about 30 or 40 more. You don't need to worry about yer quarantining, cause the smell will help keep folks away. Cept of course Erlene. If she shows up trying to take one of yore cats, jest aim a shot gun to the air, and fire off some rounds like I do when she comes sniffing around my canning cellar for peach jam. She'll leave soon enough.

Yers,
Crabigail

CR•ED

CHAPTER 30
SOME MOM

Ashley hid in an alley from the reporters. She'd had enough, and she was getting sick. Her babies had been murdered. Police said that she couldn't see them. The crime scene was terrible, they said. She needed a fix, bad.

Earlier at the precinct, they kept her sitting on a bench for hours, ignoring her. She'd overheard someone say that the murderer cut out her girls' eyes. Their beautiful green eyes. Why would he do that? She began to cry loudly. Finally, an officer said he'd drive her home, but home was the streets, and he knew it. He'd simply walked her outside and shut the door. There had been reporters everywhere. She ran then, had to. Had to get away.

Ashley tried to focus on getting her meth. She had no money, and tricks were getting harder to pull off as she was pushing fifty. To the Johns, she looked much older. Atlanta was full of younger, healthier girls ready to give it up for a little blow or some cash.

She had visions she couldn't shake off . . . a river of blood with Summer and Autumn floating on their backs, green eyes still there, open, staring at nothing, at the sun.

She slipped from doorway to doorway until she got to her favorite Pee Lab. Drug dealers in the poorer neighborhoods around had taken to opening these labs. Seems they figured out that Meth users lost about thirty percent of their drugs in their urine. So, they'd pay them $10 to pee in a jar.

The Pee Lab owners would take the urine and pour it into condoms. There was science at work here. Something about the latex condom reacting to the meth laced pee. They would tie the condoms off with string and hang them from the ceiling. After a few weeks the meth would crystalize and float to the top, and they would cut them loose, and harvest the drug.

The Pee Labs were a hit with users like Ashley. Easy money, and for doing what? Peeing? Problem was they got raided regularly and so you had to stay up on where they relocated to.

Police didn't like raiding Meth houses. If they did, their precinct was responsible for the clean-up, and these were poor areas. Cleaning up a Meth house could cost upwards of fifty grand. But, cleaning up a Pee Lab cost virtually nothing. It was just a matter of cutting down and disposing of the condoms. Pee Labs didn't have dangerous chemicals onsite like Meth houses. So, the police turned the Meth houses over to the Feds, and let them handle those raids. They'd focus on the Pee Labs, which were springing up everywhere.

Ashley squatted over her jar. The dark skinned man held it between her legs. Her ragged panties with the rotted crotch were around her ankles. The man was getting impatient as she was straining without much success, just a trickle so far.

"Listen, Bitch, I'm giving you one more minute before I throw you out of here."

Ashley nodded and finally felt the warm stream, and heard the sound of her pee filling the jar. The man handed her the ten, and placed the jar on a table filled with other jars and Pee Lab supplies. Ashley held the money for a few seconds, and then gave the ten right back to him. The man exchanged the money for a baggy with a rock. This was the way it was done. This was good Atlanta business best practices, and it was trendy. Reuse, Repurpose, Recycle.

Minutes later, in an alley beside a garbage can reeking of spoiled chicken, crack pipe in one hand, her daughters forgotten, Ashley was blissfully at peace.

ଔ•ଓ

CHAPTER 31
CORONER'S REPORTS

Agent Candor asked Ryan to join him in his room, a floor below the one he and all the twins were sharing. He handed Ryan a beer, and gesturing toward the desk chair, invited him to sit. Jim took note of the file in Ryan's hand.

"What you got there, Ryan?"

"It's the Coroner's reports. I thought I'd . . ."

"Man. You've been over those things dozens of times."

"I know. I feel ridiculous going over them and over them. I don't know what I'm supposed to be doing here. I don't have Quantico training. I'm not a detective. I'm a Rookie cop. I half understand what I'm reading anyway."

"You see a pattern, Ryan?"

"No. Not really. I do get that he started with limbs, but then didn't take them. He took those girls' eyes, though . . . why? And, why the father's ashes? It makes no sense." Ryan tossed the file on the desk and sipped his beer.

"I have something to show you." Jim pulled out a yellow manila envelope and opened the flap. He slid out a large photograph image and slid it in front of Ryan. Ryan could see a handsome blond man with chiseled movie star features.

"Who is this?"

"It's nobody, or maybe somebody."

"Huh?"

"This is a phenotype. This is the image the FBI labs have produced from pulling apart and assembling the DNA found on the vics."

"No way!" Ryan picked up the photo and studied it closely. "You gonna show it to the twins?"

"I don't know, yet. Possibly. I'm resistant. Still, some of them have some amazing instincts. What if they connect somehow? Gotta think on it, sleep on it, and run it by some higher ups. What would you do?"

"I would show them."

Jim Candor nodded and clicked his beer can against Ryan's. Then he reached over and picked up the stack of Coroner's reports and tossed them into Ryan's lap.

 CR•EO

Dear Crabigail,

I forgot my girlfriend's birthday, and want to make it up to her by giving her a necklace or a ring. Do girls still prefer diamonds, or should I consider an emerald?

Sincerely Yours,
Lover Boy in Liverpool

Dear Loser Boy,

A little history lesson fer ya: It was way back in the Stone Age, when the first caveman fergot to bring his wife home a wooly mammoth coat for her birthday. He had fergot to check the scratchins on the wall which was how they told the days. So, he ran outside and grabbed her a rock cause that's what he thought she said she wanted. If that caveman had a listened up, he'd a knowed she jest wanted one of them fancy cushioned rocking chairs, and he wouldn't ve a knot on his noggin.

Yers,
Crabigail

ᏣᎦ•ᏚᎤ

Dear Loser Boy's Girlfriend,
Get him a calendar for his birthday.

Yers,
Crabigail

ᏣᎦ•ᏚᎤ

CHAPTER 32
TATER

Tater sat at his dual computers, desk lamp swirling dust dancers around his head. Geo Earth was on one screen, zoomed into the yard of a set of twins he'd been researching all night. On the other screen was a dark web chat in multi-colored fonts scrolling so fast it was hard to keep up with the discussion. These were his friends. Conspiracy theorists that shared news of the real world . . . a world where murders were scripted from Aliens . . . a world where John F. Kennedy, Jr. and Elvis still lived in hiding, executing whores at night for unspeakable crimes . . . a world where men like Tater made the rules.

A screeching noise overhead made him stop mid typing.

"MA! Stop dragging chairs up there."

The basement door opened, and the heavy smoker yelling voice of his mother rolled down the wooden steps. "This battery ain't gonna change itself. I asked you all day to come up here and do it. If I break a hip climbing on this chair to reach it, that'll be on you."

Tater mumbled under his breath, "I'll break more than that, old lady."

"What's that? Did you hear what I said? "

"I heard you, Ma. I told you I'd get to it."

"This beeping is driving me mad. If you ain't gonna change it when I ask, I might as well take it down and throw it in the trash. Then, we can just burn alive when the house sets fire."

"I said, I'm coming. Just give me a minute."

"And bring those dirty dishes up. I ain't calling the roach guy again this week."

Tater stuffed the rest of his bologna with cheese and mustard on white bread sandwich into his mouth."

"Did you hear me?"

Tater couldn't answer right away. His mouth was full. He took a swig of Dr. Pepper from a two-liter bottle, and wiped his mouth with the hem of his t-shirt.

"TATER!"

"I HEARD YOU!"

The basement door slammed closed.

Tater hit send on the untraceable rerouted text message he'd sent to the newest twins. Pretty girls with short brown hair. Lived in Paulding County near where he'd grown up. He'd hated it there. He looked at the dirty plates and cups and the empty pizza boxes and Dorito bags. Work, more important than housekeeping, was just a mouse click away.

More noise. Louder this time.

"TATER!" This time a screech.

"I'M COMING, DAMMIT!"

The door above the steps opened again pouring light so bright it drowned out the dust bunnies. Men in black with ball caps reading FBI came running down with guns drawn and orders to "DON'T MOVE" and "HANDS IN THE AIR WHERE WE CAN SEE THEM."

As Tater was led up the stairs in handcuffs, he could hear over his mother's sobs, the fire alarm beeping.

CR•SO

Dear Crabigail,

My husband wants me to join him at a nudist colony. I have a pretty good figure, so I don't mind being naked, but I wonder what kind of activities they have at a place like that.

Sincerely,
Size Four in Fort Knox

Dear Needs a Biscuit or Two,

I reckon them nudey places got the same kinds of activities as any other resort. They probably got putt putt, and bike riding, and skeet shooting. Only if you go to the firing range, I'd tote me a garbage can lid and hold it down at my hoo hoo, so I don't get myself shot in the grassy knoll.

Yers,
Crabigail

 CR• SO

CHAPTER 33
TWIXES, DIET COKES, AND DNA

Since the cheapskate government emptied out our minibars of everything except warm bottled water, Pam and I joined the Miller twin's raid on the over-priced hallway snack machine. We had enough quarters and smooth one dollar bills between us all to purchase two Diet Cokes and three bags of popcorn. Pam's Twix bar was sadly left dangling between the Honey Buns and Ranch Doritos. I shook the machine trying to dislodge the candy, and when that didn't work, Pam used her wheelchair as a battering ram, but the Twix refused to fall. Pam can be ferocious when she weaponizes her chair. She met her match with the Twix though, gave up, and settled with sharing my popcorn.

The other twins retired to their rooms a couple of hours earlier, after we were abruptly hurried out of our information session by Officer Ryan. Something had obviously come up, because an aide whispered into his ear, and handed him a cell phone. We watched him listen wide-eyed to the caller and say, "Yes, Sir. I'll be there in forty-five minutes . . . Yes, Sir . . . Yes, Sir." He handed the phone back to the aide.

"Ladies. I'm sorry, but we'll have to cut this short today. You'll need to return to your rooms with Officer Lynn." Ryan nodded at the officer standing by the door who beckoned for us to follow her. We did as we were told, but of course we were dying of curiosity. Before we could ask anything, though, he was out the door and gone.

The Miller twins brought their purchases to our room, and we plopped on my bed chatting, and sharing snacks. We watched what turned out to be a favorite movie for all four of us, Patrick Swayze's "Dirty Dancing." Pam moved from her wheelchair to her own bed, and was still pouting over the Twix bar.

"It's the principal of the thing, not the money. I think it's a deliberate scam by the snack machine company."

"Yep, you're right, Pam. The CEO of Stale Foods Unlimited is sitting in his office, as we speak, giggling and rubbing his hands over the seventy-five cents he can add to his millions."

"I'm just saying!" Pam would have the last word, no matter what.

Delanie was amused, but thought it wise to change the subject. "So, Penny, You're an artist and an author, right? That must be so fun."

"That's true. I like to be creative."

"What kind of books do you write? Are you published?"

Pam interrupted. "She writes bodice-ripping trashy love stories.

"No. I don't."

"Yes, she does." Pam cleared her throat so she could fake quote me. I had no idea where she was going with this.

"She writes stuff like, *Blake gazed lustfully upon the mossy valley from whence all pleasure flows.*"

Delanie and Savannah giggled.

"I have NEVER written anything like that!"

Pam's mood was definitely improving. "Here's another one: *As she kissed her way down his manly chest, Virginia's petticoats dropped to the floor, rustling like a cockroach in a sugar bowl.*"

The redheads were howling now.

"Stop it," I insisted, but she was on a roll, and there was no stopping her.

Her breasts heaved like a stormy ocean, erupting with the foam of desire.

"I swear I'm gonna kill you."

I would give Delanie a copy of "Bearing Crosses," later, so she could see Pam was making all that up. I had to admit though, I kind of liked the rustling cockroach imagery. I was thinking about how I could use it in a story, when we heard a knock.

Savannah opened the door, and looked through the chain at Officer Ryan. He came to fetch us all to return to the conference room, or maybe for dinner. It was about that time anyway, and despite the popcorn, I was a little hungry. The others were in the hallway. We joined them, and went downstairs as a group. Pam was feeling pretty frisky after her adrenaline boost of besting me, and left her chair behind, pushing her walker instead. Good for her, I thought, but I'm still gonna kill her later.

Ryan had Officer Lynn escort us so that he could go on ahead. When we entered the room, he was standing in front of a large TV with Agent Candor.

"Ladies." That was Agent Candor's way of greeting us, and we all said hello to him. We hadn't seen him in a couple of days. I guess he'd been off solving crimes. Hopefully, finding the serial killer, so we could go home.

"Ladies, please have a seat. Dinner will arrive in a bit, but I . . . we . . . need to go over a few things with you."

Agent Candor told us some guy named Eugene Franklin, known to his friends and family as "Tater," had been arrested. He's the guy who sent us all the horrible messages. It seems he'd done all his terrorizing from his mother's basement, and was absolutely not the murderer. DNA had cleared him.

Watching the news, fascinated with the grim stories of murdered twins, Tater became obsessed. Others in his online world were just as interested, and a loose assortment of late night misfits formed a sordid chat group. On a "what if" dare from one of his dark web buddies, Tater located dozens of pairs of female twins in Georgia. He used tracking devices to pinpoint where the twins were and geo earth sites to view locations. It was very insidious. I was amazed that he could find his way to Lizzie's phone and see aerial views of her property. Ewww! Big Brother wasn't the only one watching.

Tater was harmless. Didn't mean he wasn't in big trouble, though. He'd face charges for making terroristic threats, and the theft and distribution of illegally-obtained movies, and whatever else they could throw at him. When the time came for him to get out of prison, he'd be banned from ever having computer access again.

Animated chatter around the room was interrupted by Agent Candor clearing his throat.

"I want to show you some images on the screen, and if any of you have seen this person feel free to speak up . . . Ryan."

Ryan turned on the TV, and using a remote, he clicked past a screen saver of the FBI logo. A man's image appeared. It didn't seem real to me, not like a photograph. It appeared to be created in a graphics program of some kind. I leaned forward. It was very well done. I would love to have a program that could create this kind of . . .

"Miss Penny. Do you recognize him?" Ryan mistook my interest in the graphics program for knowledge.

I tried to concentrate on the image itself. A handsome blond-haired man with a beautiful Grecian nose. Not at all what I would think a serial killer would look like. "Sorry, Officer Ryan. I have no idea who that man is. Who is he?"

Agent Candor spoke, "Anyone? Do any of you ladies recognize this man?"

No one did. Jakis raised her hand, "Who's that supposed to be?"

"Is that Tater?" Delanie asked.

"Can't be Tater," replied Savannah. "Does he look like a Tater? Nobody that looks like that is gonna be living in his mother's basement. This guy is hot!"

"Ladies. This is a phenotype, not an actual photograph. FBI labs have" . . . my brain scrambled a bit as the agent went on to give us a five minute lecture on DNA that none of us understood . . . "and we think this might very well be a good representation of what our perp may look like."

"No kidding!" I couldn't help my reaction. "I didn't know that was something you guys could do."

Jakis was the first to say what we were all thinking. "Ain't nobody that good looking gonna be a killer."

Jacqueline shook her head. "Ted Bundy was good looking, too. Look what he did."

Pam said nothing. She had that contemplative look that I recognized. I'm not a mind reader like her, but I knew she was sticking to her guns with her belief that the killer was a woman.

I asked for her. "Is it possible that there are two? A man and a woman working together?"

Agent Candor nodded. "Anything's possible. I'm just wondering if any of you have an impression from this image, a feeling, anything at all."

We all shook our heads, no. Still, we were transfixed by the image on the screen.

The FBI agent looked disappointed as he pulled up a chair, and sat down across from Pam and me. "DNA. The possibilities of what we can achieve with a tiny amount of DNA continue to improve every day. We have the ability to project the probable eye color, hair color and texture, skin tone, height and weight of a subject. We can tell the shape of the chin and cheek bones and the height of the forehead. Amazing stuff, really."

"I'll say!" Savannah said. "That's just crazy."

Pam leaned forward. "So you think this looks like the killer. You can tell, not just that it's a man, but that it's THIS man." While we all bought in that this handsome man was the murderer they sought, Pam had not.

"Yes, Ma'am. We won't know how close we've gotten until we catch him. I was hoping one of you had seen him before."

Lureen spoke up. "Would you mind leaving that on the screen while we eat? Let us live with it awhile? Maybe something will come to one of us."

"I certainly can do that. You ladies enjoy your dinner. I hear you are having Maryland Crab Cakes. Make sure you try the remoulade sauce."

"Yum." Delanie seemed more interested in dinner now than the killer.

"Study his face well through dinner. If you ever do see him, we'll need to know right away."

Jakis slapped the table. "You ain't gotta worry about that Agent Candor."

We ate and chatted and did our usual carrying on, but we all returned our attention to the man on the screen every few minutes. Agent Candor was right about the crab cakes and the sauce. Delicious! When Pam dropped her napkin, I reached down to pick it up. I caught my breath. The image of the blond man from that odd angle came into view from my peripheral. Something was suddenly familiar about him, but I couldn't quite grasp it. I sat up slowly and looked again. Nothing. I turned my head slightly so that I was looking from the side again. What was it? Someone I've seen. Think.

I slid my little spiral notebook from the pocket of my purse and started looking back through my notes . . . page after page. There it was. I remembered the picture I saw in the Records Room. The man on the screen was considerably older than the man from the pictures in the files in Robbie's office, but it was him. He was the man, Adam Fitzgerald, a doctor whose doctor wife, while pregnant with twins, had pounded a spike into his head, many years ago.

CR•EO

Dear Crabigail,

I always go places my wife wants to go to, but she shows no interest in doing the same for me. I asked her to go with me to the drag races on Saturday, and she said, "No, because WE have volunteered to take puppies from the shelter to be spayed and neutered." Do you think this is fair?

Sincerely Asking,
Dragless in Daytona

Dear Drag Ass,

I'd go if I was her, cause I love the drag racing. A few years ago John Earl started coming home late and smelling funny. I threatened to set his keester on fire with a burning broom if he didn't tell me what he was up to, so he blurted out he'd been at a drag show. I was real mad then, cause I'd rather be there than stuck at home with yungins, so he promised to take me. Next Saturday evening, I put on my Dale Earnhardt t-shirt, my Dale Earnhardt hat, my Dale Earnhardt boots, my ruby red lipstick, and hopped in the truck with John Earl. We drove way out of town to some place. There weren't no race track, weren't no cars, and weren't no Dale Earnhardt. All I saw were a bunch of made up floozies with their boobs hanging out. Only show that night was me chasing John Earl with a burning broom.

Yers,
Crabigail

അ•ഓ

CHAPTER 34
SOMEBODY'S JAM DONE SLID OFF THEIR BISCUIT

After sharing my information about the doctor with Agent Candor and Officer Ryan, we were all whisked off to our rooms. We were told our dessert would be delivered later by room service.

I left Pam alone in the room to find a place to call Lizzie and Dan. My sister was napping and I slipped out quietly. Pam was worn out from the entire trip, and we hadn't been able to do one bit of sightseeing. I'd bring her back one day, and we'd do the whole city right including every single Smithsonian Museum.

I walked as far down the hallway as I could from our FBI guard. The man had to be a former Marine. He was so stoic. Never smiled, never made conversation with any of us. I stopped by the big picture window overlooking the Capitol building.

I called Lizzie first. I wanted to fill her in on the whole Tater in the basement business, but didn't need to after all.

"I know all about it. Guy sounds pathetic."

"What do you mean you know all about it? I didn't think they'd released that to the press yet."

"Agent Candor . . . Jim called me, and filled me in."

"He did? That's kind of odd. Don't you think?"

"No. He's a good-looking man. I'm a good-looking, gorgeous actually, woman. Why wouldn't he call me?"

"I would just think that, with a serial killer on the loose, he might have better things to do than to call you. No offense."

"None taken. Hey, I gotta run. Getting my nails done, you know, just in case."

"Lord."

I called Dan next.

"Hey. It's me."

"Hey, back atcha."

I filled him in on my contribution, identifying the picture of the Doctor, and how the FBI agents were scrambling afterwards, and had hustled us back to our rooms with no dessert. I told him how the crab cakes had bacon in them, and that I hoped they caught the guy soon so I could make him some. I also told him about the Tater Tot weirdo. He was relieved that the threat on Lizzie's phone was nothing to worry about.

The conversation shifted to Dan's problems, and the fact that my husband had lost his jam, and not in a physical, psychological, or philosophical way. He'd truly lost his jam, specifically ten jars of blackberry and strawberry jam Pam made him for his birthday. What happened was, last summer, Pam, who is family-famous for her home-made jams, reached the point where she was making somewhere around twenty varieties such as strawberry, peach, apple butter, cherry, muscadine, apricot, and blackberry. Some jars held combinations of the fruit. She goes to a lot of trouble picking the berries out at the local farmers market and harvesting her own peach tree, peeling, cutting, and cooking the fruit, boiling jars, and sealing them properly. Now that she's disabled, I should encourage her to stop, but I can't, because quite frankly, you can't buy jam this delicious.

Instead of doling out a few pints to her beloved family at Christmas, Pam switched to tiny little quarter-pints adorned with her own label bearing a caricature of her face and cute jam names like *Peachy Keen* and *Bohemian Grape Seedy*, and all labeled *Pam Jam*. I thought her solution was marvelous. The sampler sizes gave us the opportunity to try all of the varied concoctions of my sister's culinary talents, and most of us were grateful.

The only disgruntled jam recipient was my husband. Dan frowned when he opened his Christmas box full of sampler Pam Jams nestled in colorful paper confetti. Thankfully, Pam didn't hear him complain.

Later, at home he showed me his gift. "What the heck is this?"

"It's your allotment of jam. Can you let Roxie outside?"

"There's like a teaspoon of jam in these tiny jars."

Dan opened the door and waited while our cat stood half in and half out, trying to decide what she wanted to do.

"Go out, Cat!"

Roxie changed her mind and ran under the dining room table.

"There's more than that. She made them quarter size so you can try them all. Wasn't that sweet?"

"It's a quarter size all right!" Dan closed the door.

Dan growled some more, but I wasn't listening, not that I could as Roxie was crowing like a rooster. I called Pam to report Dan, and to see if she would adopt our seventeen-year-old mentally ill cat when we retire and move to the beach in South Carolina.

"Hey."

"Hey. No, I'm not taking your cat when you move to Myrtle Beach."

"Okay. I wasn't calling about that, but why wouldn't you? Roxie's a little neurotic, but she sleeps most of the day and . . ."

"No."

"There's coyotes where we're moving, and how do you do that?"

"No. How do I do what?"

"How do you know what I'm calling about before I say what I'm calling about?"

"I don't know. I just know. Is your cat crowing again?"

"Yes. Dan was trying to make her go outside. It's what she does. So, do you know the other reason I was calling?"

"No."

"I'll give you a hint. It has to do with your jam."

"Oh. You're welcome."

Thankfully, my twin isn't prescient all the time.

"Dan's fussing about the little sampler jars. Says he only gets a teaspoon of jam."

Pam laughed. "Okay, for starters there are twenty jars in the box instead of his usual ten, and there is at least a half cup of jam in each jar."

"That's what I told him. DAN! PAM SAYS FOR YOU TO QUIT WHINING!"

"Listen. Tell him I'll make it up to him on his birthday."

So April came, and Dan received a big box with ten full pints of jam: five blackberry and five strawberry, from my sister. Since our pantry was already well stocked with jam, I assumed he stored it away somewhere. Now, months later, he's on the phone telling me that he can't find any of it.

"I don't understand. You opened the box, and I took a picture of you holding all ten jars. You put the picture on Facebook. What did you do with the box after that?"

"I put the box beside my chair. That's the last place I saw it, and I haven't seen it since. We had so much jam stocked up from before, I haven't looked for my birthday jam until now."

"I know you aren't blaming me."

"Well . . ."

"I did NOT hide your jam."

"I got my birthday jam, and then left the next day for the Masters. You had your girls' weekend then, right?"

"So?"

"That's the last time I saw it."

"So?"

"I'm just saying."

"Lord."

"Ask your sister if she took it back."

"You think Pam stole her own jam back from you?"

"I'm not saying 'stole' . . . not exactly. Just ask her."

We finished the call with 'love yous,' and I promised to stay safe. I couldn't wait to tell Pam about Dan's crazy jam conspiracy theory.

I opened the door to our room, and could see Pam wasn't on the bed. Her wheelchair sat empty. My eyes began to adjust from the bright hallway. I saw her. Pam was face down on the floor by the window, not moving.

ೞ•ഓ

CHAPTER 35
BACK TO APRIL

Ryan listened while Agent Candor was on the phone. The FBI with the GBI and local law enforcement had boots on the ground in Atlanta at North Peachtree Rehabilitation Hospital where Adam Fitzgerald had resided for years. Ryan couldn't hear the other side, but he gleaned enough to note that the agents were saying it was impossible for the patient to get out of his bed and do anything.

Jim filled him in afterwards. "It seems that, when his wife drove the spike into his head, she actually used her hand to manipulate it. As a neurosurgeon, April Fitzgerald knew just how to maneuver the spike to ensure her husband existed in a vegetative state for the rest of his life. The doctors say there is just no way he is sneaking out of his room and killing people. Still, they allowed us to take saliva samples. We'll get a report soon enough."

Ryan was puzzled. "So if the DNA matches, but it's not possible for him to really do anything, what then?"

"I don't know, Ryan. It's strange."

"What about the wife. What happened to her?"

"Seems she was mentally ill, and no one saw it. She worked as a neurosurgeon. Can you imagine? Anyway, she was pregnant at the time with twins. Coincidence? I have Robbie sending over the whole case file."

Jim noticed the file in Ryan's hand. "Are you still reading the Coroner's Reports? You should have them memorized by now."

Ryan looked embarrassed but looked Jim dead in the eye. "I'm not sure, sir, but I think I might have found something. Not sure if it's important, but maybe it's something."

"Go ahead."

Trying to show a confidence he didn't feel, Ryan said, "So, I noticed in the pictures the incisions are real clean. The Coroner thinks a hunting knife not a scalpel. We talked about that." He looked up at the agent.

Agent Candor nodded and Ryan continued.

"If you look at these pictures where the limbs were severed, there is a small v cut on the edge of the incision like a tiny piece was removed. It's like a small missing jigsaw piece. It's like that on all of them. And now, he's taken the eyes from the last victims. I think it means something."

Agent Candor leaned forward. "What do you think it means, Ryan? Do you think he's taking trophies, building a Frankenstein? What?"

"I don't know exactly. The pieces are so small; the Coroner thinks with a hunting knife. I think it's something else. Other than the eyes, nothing removed's been, you know, very big. Maybe we could ask the twins, the ones with psychic abilities."

Jim examined the cuts Ryan had circled in the pictures and nodded. "I think you're right, Ryan. I think these are definitely v sections removed. Small, but precise. Usually, when this type of serial killer takes a trophy it's more, how do I say this . . . significant. Maybe we should . . ."

He was interrupted with a knock on the door. It was the courier with the Armstrong file and their attention immediately shifted.

Agent Candor frowned. "The wife is dead. April Fitzgerald was sent to a mental hospital to await the birth of her twins. She seemed to do well there. The staff found her to be calm and lucid; no different than her colleagues where she had been a resident. In her ninth month, it seems she got hold of a knife, and attempted to perform her own cesarean. She died, and one of the infants did as well."

"Good Lord." Ryan couldn't believe a mother could do that to herself.

"She did. Bled out. The medical staff managed to save one of the babies. A little girl."

"What happened to the baby?"

"Doesn't say. I imagine she was put up for adoption or sent to foster care, maybe family. We'll check into that. It's been twenty-five years."

Ryan mulled that over.

"Ryan, I know you wanted to talk to them more, but for now, it's time to send the twins home."

CR•EO

Dear Crabigail,

I am freezing! My feet feel like popsicles. Any advice to warm a girl up?

Signed,
Chilly in Chile

Dear Take a Chill Pill,

You interrupting my Soaps for that? Who cares? I got problems of my own self. I'm hankering right now for a grilled cheese with Velveeta and I'm plum outa white bread. Last thing I wanna be thinking on when I'm hungry is yore nasty feet.

Yers,
Crabigail

☙•❧

CHAPTER 36
LOST A PERFECTLY GOOD CUP OF SWEET TEA

Dropping my cup of tea on the tile floor I ignored the explosion of beverage and Styrofoam, and ran to my sister. "Pam! Pam! Are you okay?" I grabbed her arm and turned her over.

"I'm fine. Leave me alone."

"What happened? Did you fall?"

She sat up, looking perturbed. "No, I didn't fall. You had the outlet between the beds tied up with your IPad charger, your Kindle, and your laptop, so I was on the floor trying to plug my phone into the outlet under the AC. While I was doing that, the AC went off and I could hear sounds coming up through the vent. Did you just spill your tea all over our room?"

"What kind of sound? You mean like a rat or a squirrel?"

"No. I could hear voices. Here." Pam tossed me a towel to clean up the tea. "So, I put my ear to the vent and was listening. It was Agent Candor and Officer Ryan talking about the case. Agent Candor . . . Shemar . . . his room must be right under ours. You missed a spot by the dresser. I was finding out all kinds of stuff when you interrupted me."

I mopped up tea listening to my sister's depravity. I was the textbook definition of aghast. "Pam! That's a terrible invasion of their privacy, and for Pete's sake! He's the FBI! You could probably go to jail for doing that. I need another towel."

"Want to know what I learned?" She pulled down the dirty towel from her morning shower, drying on the back of a chair, and threw it to me.

"No, I certainly do not." Finished, I tossed both of the towels into the bathroom.

She tilted her head like a "nystagmic chicken" and stared at me.

"Okay, go ahead."

While I fished one more ice cube from under the dresser, Pam told me about April Fitzgerald and about her pregnancy with twins, ending with the one baby surviving.

"That's horrible. You and I have both had babies. Can you imagine taking a knife to your own abdomen?" I picked up the pieces of Styrofoam and a few stray ice cubes.

"Not hardly. Course I don't feel pain, but still even I couldn't do something so horrid."

"Pam. What do you think it means? To the case . . . what does it mean?"

"It happened twenty-five years ago. It's karma, like you finding out about killing my dog, Judy, and then rescuing those fish. It's the daughter killing twins. I just know it. Karma says we were meant to know it." She used her foot to push the plastic lid and straw my direction.

"Karma doesn't work like that and you know it. You really think the murderer is the child . . . . the daughter . . . of the doctors?" I flicked the lid and straw into the wastebasket.

"I'm as certain of that as I am that Dan is going to call you in a few minutes to tell you he found his missing jam."

Once I was sure the floor was dry and not slippery, I helped Pam up off the floor.

She said, "Oh by the way, they're sending us home tomorrow."

Just then, my phone rang. It was Dan. He'd found his jam. Lord.

CR•ED

CHAPTER 37
STOP HER

Diana's head hurt, and she was worried about her twin. She hadn't heard from her sister all day. Depression was setting in, and she counted on her sister to fight off the effects. She would take a long hot bath. That would help.

Diana and Paul were shower people. They had been all of their three years of living together. Early on, they lost their bathtub stopper and, because they were shower people, they never cared to replace it. Paul looked for it once when he was trying to put a bunch of trout he'd caught on ice in the tub. He asked Diana how a round rubber bathroom stopper with a metal pull ring just up and disappears? She shrugged and said, "Maybe you mistook it for a fishing bobber." Paul just laughed and hugged her. He liked it when she was funny. Most days Diana was morose and going on and on about her sister, and he wasn't sure he could take much more of that. She wasn't about to tell him the truth about the missing stopper . . . why she threw it away. Thankfully, Paul forgot all about it. Her moods got to him, though. He took to volunteering more and more for the longer truck routes. Diana found things to do while he was gone. Projects.

Now, Diana had a headache, and she was depressed, and that set her to pondering a hot, soaking bath. Waves of sadness showered down around her from the top of her blond hair to the end of her chipped Sassy Scarlet acrylic toenails. Her chest tightened in intermittent, crushing vice-like blows. It wasn't painful physically, but the intense pressure was awful all the same. She had some regrets about the stopper.

Diana had already taken her prescribed Bupropion and Duloxetine. They were generic for famous drugs that were advertised everyday on TV that she could never remember the name of. One was for depression and the other anxiety . . . Not sure which was which. She took two and waited. Some days the meds kept her even. But that day, like other bad days, they didn't. She dug through her cabinet and found the Xanax she'd stolen from her aunt, the one who raised her. She waited an hour. Like the others, it didn't work either.

She thought about calling Paul . . . letting him talk her through it, but he was driving his rig through some bad stormy weather up north in Worcester, Mass. She didn't want to distract him. Plus, he would want to badger her about what triggered her depression, and she couldn't answer that exactly. He would say, "What happened, Diana? Something must have happened to make you feel this way." What he wouldn't do is tell her to talk to her twin. He'd turn his rig around and come straight home, driving fast on wet, slick roads. She didn't want that, either. Depression always hit hard, out of the blue, and for no sensible reason that she could explain, that would make any sense to her boyfriend. A hot bath . . . that would stop it.

Diana thought of stuffing the drain with a wadded washcloth, but she couldn't guarantee that it would hold a tub full of warm water. So, she drove to the Dollar Store up on Main Street near where Winn Dixie used to be. She didn't know why people in the South gave directions by where things were before, but they did. She imagined when she died, they'd say "Diana's body's buried over yonder where that big Sassafras tree used to be . . . the one that leaned over the road til the power folks chopped her down. You know! It's a bit down to the left from where Mabel used to raise them goats in that pen that got swallowed up by the tornado."

In the store she combed the aisles looking for stoppers. Someone she knew came in. It was her neighbor, Medra Maxwell. Diana knew she couldn't talk to anyone that day and most certainly not to bubbly Medra. Diana avoided her neighbor by hiding out in a back aisle looking at soap products. She picked up a box. Her bubbles would come from a Calgon box, not mindless, cheerful conversation.

She could barely see and hear Medra up front looking at ceramic frogs with solar lighted huge eyes. She could see the top of Medra's frosty brown hair she'd more than likely just had done over at the Cut and Clip. She was saying to an employee, "Aren't these frogs just the cutest things? Did I teach you in schoo'? Who's your people? Do I know em? You look like a Miller. Are you a Miller? Did you graduate from Douglas High Schoo'? Oh, you went to Grady?"

Diana had seen them, too . . . the big eyed solar frogs . . . when she came in, but ignored them on her quest for a bathtub stopper. "This will be fabulous in my garden," Medra laughed. "Look at his great big eyes. He's got some character in him." Diana assumed she was talking to the girl at the register now. She waited and waited for Medra to leave until she finally heard silence. Silence had a cadence all its own.

She left her hiding spot and crept around the corner to where she'd once seen some kitchen gadgets. From there, she could see the register, but no Medra. Diana found the stopper on the bottom shelf next to some misplaced no-name-brand green beans that didn't even have a pull top, and behind a stack of black electrical tape. She carried the stopper and bubble bath to the register, and on a whim, snapped up her own solar-eyed ugly frog. With tax, her purchase came to three dollars and twenty-one cents.

The clouds were heavier than when she left home. At the red light, while her blinker blinked right, she looked up at them. "Go ahead and rain why don't ya?" Her twin sister always loved a good rainstorm, even thunder and lightning, but pending rain weighed heavy on Diana like piles of rocks. Her Doctor said it was a reaction to changes in the barometric pressure. The light took forever. With her left hand on the steering wheel, Diana began tapping her chest, forehead and cheeks with her fingers, a technique she researched on Google. *Tap, tap, tap.* Amazing how it loosened the tightness, if only temporary.

Home at last, Diana changed into her favorite pink robe. It smelled like Downy and cigarettes and Paul. She smoked half a Winston out the bathroom window as she waited for the tub to fill. She turned the water off at the halfway point so that she had some wiggle room to add hotter water as her body adjusted to the temperature. Diana dropped the partially smoked cigarette into the toilet and flushed it, watching to make sure it properly swirled away. Paul was forever asking her not to flush them, as he thought for sure they clogged up the septic. He was probably right. She closed the lid.

From the closet, she removed all of the bath oil and bubble bath gift sets Paul gave her for various occasions, and opened them, lining the pretty bottles and the Calgon all along the edge of the tub. She took a brand new pink Lady razor from her shelf above the sink, and laid it on the edge of the tub between the Pier One Croustade Aux Pommes and the Bath and Body Works Milk and Honey. She hadn't bothered getting a towel because she wouldn't need one, but she did wrap her head in a terry cloth turban that fastened in the front with a loop and a wedge of bamboo.

This will make me feel better. Maybe better than doing the other thing. Sis will be disappointed. My head hurts so bad.

Diana touched the tepid water with her fingers and turned the faucet on again to add a little more hot. From the deep pockets of her robe, she took out the Dollar Tree frog. She covered the solar panel with a couple of Band-Aids from the bathroom drawer to fool it into thinking it was dark. Sure enough, his eyes glowed brightly and she sat him on the closed toilet seat lid. Beside him, she laid her cellphone.

Pockets now empty, she let her robe puddle to the tile floor and slid into the tub, knocking the razor into the water. She fished it out and laid it on the toilet, dripping, next to her phone and the glowing eyed frog. As Diana adjusted to the warmth, she sank lower in the water. Her hair turban served as a cushion against the icy cold tile above the tub. With her left foot, she tried to turn off the hot water, but couldn't. She sat up and used her hand to turn the knob to a trickle.

She began opening bottles. One was an Estee Lauder Bubble Bath with a mango, lemon scent. She poured it all in, and then tried her best to foam it up by fishtailing her hands vigorously back and forth. When this didn't work, she turned the hot water on full and mixed in a little of the cold, so that the stream battered down on the floating goo. That did the trick, and soon she was having to bat towering pillars of foam away from her face. She smiled for the first time in a week.

Squeezing her eyes tight and sliding down in the water, Diana breathed deeply. She began tapping her chest again. *Tap, Tap, Tap.* Then her forehead. *Tap, Tap, Tap.* She sat up suddenly, knocking three bottles off the edge to the floor. She grabbed the frog and smashed down hard on the Lady Razor. Plastic flew everywhere, but the frog didn't suffer so much as a crack. Diana brushed aside the broken plastic pieces and pulled out one of the three little razors.

She held the razor blade in her right hand, and used her left to continue tapping. *Tap, Tap, Tap.* She felt herself calm, and leaned her turbaned head on the tile, and began taking deep breaths. She stopped tapping and held her arm under the warm water. Just a puncture, a small puncture to see what it would feel like. She cut into the little scar from before . . . from when she'd thrown the stopper away. The pain made her wince, but wasn't too bad yet. She'd certainly felt worse. Diana pushed away the foam, and watched a tiny rivulet of blood snake its way down around her belly, settling into some of the stretch marks, making them redder than they already were. *I can do this*, she thought. *Just as easy as cutting up a buck.* She lowered the blade into the water to the same spot.

Her phone rang. She dropped the razor in the water where it sank to the bottom between her legs. She sat up, and with a foamy hand answered it. It was her twin calling.

"Hey, Sis."

This is an important message about your car's warranty.

"I don't feel very good."

Your car warranty has expired . . .

"Glad you called."

To extend coverage press one . . .

"I'm having a bad day again. I'm in that place in my head."

This is a final courtesy call . . .

"Sweet of you to call. You always know what to say to make me feel better. But, I can't go back out today. I don't feel good. You'll have to hunt without me."

With foamy fingers and blood running down her wrist to her elbow she tried to change the subject, "Tell me something funny."

The phone had gone dead.

"Nothing, huh? Well, I got one for you."

Silence

"A weasel walks into a bar. The bartender looks up and says, 'Wow! In all my years tending bar, I've never had a weasel stop by. What can I get you?'"

A beep sounded the end of the recorded message.

"Give up, Sis? He says, 'Pop, Goes the Weasel?' Get it?" Diana laughed hard.

"I could have asked, 'What happens to a weasel when you fill it with too much helium?" Again, she laughed, slapping at the water as she did so.

The chat with her sister made her feel better, but the water was turning cold and her skin was starting to prune.

"Hey, Sis. I'll talk to you later. Gonna make things right for both of us soon. I promise. Soon as I feel better. This was fun." She laid the phone back on the toilet lid.

Diana used her toe, hooked the ring, and successfully dislodged the stopper. Her robe was warm, and absorbent, and helpful since she hadn't brought a towel. She wrapped her wet, naked body in it, and tied the sash securely. She scraped the bits of plastic still on the toilet lid, and the pieces from the floor, into the wastebasket along with the razor. She added the open bath oils on top, and stored the rest in the closet. She removed the bag, tied it securely, and carried it to the outside dumpster.

Her wrist was still trickling blood. Returning through the kitchen door, she wrapped her arm in a dishcloth, and went back to the bathroom. Diana pulled both Band-Aids from the frog's solar panel and put them over the tiny little nick, stopping the bleeding. As she turned off the light, the frog's eyes lit up again, shining directly on the plug sitting on the edge of the tub. She picked the stopper up and looked at it for a second and put it in her pocket. She walked to the door and stopped, returning to take the frog from the toilet seat. "My sister will love him."

She found a small gift bag on the top shelf of her bedroom closet and dropped the frog in. She'd give it to her sister for their birthday. The stopper she hid in the top of the hall closet next to her and Paul's hunting gear for the next time. It fit nicely by the sharp hunting knife. This time, she wouldn't throw the stopper away. She was pretty sure she'd need it again.

CR•ED

CHAPTER 38
TO INFINITY AND HOME

The flight home was a breeze. Pam had completely gotten over her flying phobia. She moved to her seat without fanfare, pulled out the new Sky Mall magazine, and began to circle a couple of possible orders. I could tell she was exhausted. The other twins were seated further back. We'd say our goodbyes when we reached Atlanta.

"You never told me where Dan found his jam."

"In the pantry. I put it there about ten minutes after he opened it back in April."

"Hmmm. I was gonna tell him thieves obviously broke in your house, and my jam was the only thing of value they could find." Pam closed the Sky Mall and rested her head on a pillow against the window.

I laughed, and then turned my attention to a ruckus beside me.

We were seated across from a mom and her teenage autistic son. The young man was having a meltdown. He was clearly fearful of the flight. He had the snack tray down and was banging his head on it, wailing. His mom rubbed his back, and said soothing things to try to calm him, but nothing helped. As the plane began to taxi, his wail became even louder. He thrashed his arms up and down. Suddenly, his mom asked, "Buddy! What does Buzz Lightyear say before he flies?" And then, she raised her arms straight up in the air. He did the same as she did. Together, they both began yelling "TO INFINITY AND BEYOND . . . TO INFINITY AND BEYOND."

Mother and son continued yelling this as the plane took off, and probably everyone could hear them, even in the back of the plane. They stopped as the plane leveled off, just as Pam had with her expletive on our first flight. The young man grinned ear to ear and said, "That was GREAT, Mom. That was just GREAT!"

I didn't know this mom, and would probably never see her again, but she WAS great. My only regret was that I didn't throw my hands up and yell with them. I wish I'd thought of it at the time, but I was caught up in the awesomeness of the moment. I looked over at Pam to see if she was smiling like the rest of the passengers. Pam, head resting against the window, slept through the whole thing.

I thought about this mom's wonderful lesson the rest of the flight. Maybe I should learn from her and find better, kinder ways to help my sister. Instead of that terrible, unsympathetic preflight list I gave to Pam, I could have bought her some soothing lavender hand lotion, or some bubble bath, or sent her some deep breathing exercises. Maybe, just maybe, I should try to be nicer to my twin. I thought about that for a few minutes and then I thought, *Nahhh*.

CR•BO

Dear Crabigail

My husband used to sing to me while we was making sweet, sweet love. But now, instead of the soft sexy tunes of Al Green or Conway Twitty, all I hear is snoring. I think he's lost his jam. What should I do?

Jamless in Seattle

Dear Jamless,

I know just what ya mean. I make the best dang gooseberry jam in Georgia, and my brother-in-law just loves it. But one day, my sister calls and says, "Bubba done lost that whole box of gooseberry jam you sent."

So I says, "Did ya look in the cabinet next to the peanut butter jar with the spoon still sticking out of it?"

"First place I looked," she says.

"Did ya look under the hood of that old Chrysler of his? You know he's always sticking his face under there to see if today's the day it's gonna blow."

"Yep," she says, "I've looked everwhere."

"Well," I tell her, "gooseberries don't grow on trees" (They do, but that don't matter none). "He ain't gitten no more."

Anyways, so a few months later she calls me and says, "Found the jam, and now I'm getting a new Maytag washing machine."

Let that be a lesson to all you ladies. Always check yer man's pockets for jam jars and what not before you do the laundry.

Yers,
Crabigail

ℭ•ℬ

CHAPTER 39
JUST STICK A FORK IN ME

Pam was unpacking in the guestroom, and I found Dan in the kitchen making turkey sandwiches. He held up a fork.

"This is the third time I've found a fork in the head of lettuce!"

"Yep."

"You put it in there on purpose?"

"I did. Now, put it back."

"Why? What's it for?"

"It's a trick Mom taught me. Stainless steel keeps the lettuce green and crispy."

"Well, I took it out last week while you were in D.C."

"Uh huh. See those brown edges on the lettuce? Your fault!"

If Dan would just Google the things I do, he wouldn't ask so many questions, and I would have better produce."

We had a lovely lunch, and a relaxing rest of the day. With Tater arrested, and Police and FBI agents outside, Dan felt more confident about my safety. He left for work the next morning, and Pam waited until he was gone to pounce. I should have seen it coming. She's about as weird as a fork in the lettuce crisper.

"Get dressed. We've got an errand to run."

"Pam, we've had a long trip. If you need something, I'm sure I've got whatever it is in a drawer somewhere."

"We are going to the Peachtree Rehabilitation Hospital to see that doctor."

"We are doing no such thing. We've done all we're doing. Let the detectives deal with it."

"I'm not sitting around here waiting on a twin killer to chop us up."

"Pam. Look outside. We have FBI agents and police officers guarding the house front and back."

"Yep, but guess where they aren't. They aren't at the side of the house, and you have a nice big window there. We can climb out. You can lower my wheelchair over the side."

"Forget about it. I'm not doing any such thing."

"Why?" Pam was truly shocked that I wouldn't crawl out a window to escape FBI agents to do . . . what?

"Why? You ask me why? What on earth do you expect to find?"

"Look, Penny. The Doctor is clearly not the murderer. No one can interview him because he's semi-comatose. If it's his daughter, she's been there. He knows her. I might be able to communicate with him, you know, in my own way."

"You are out of your mind."

"True, but what if?"

"What if? What if we get ourselves killed?"

"I've got an Uber on the way." She looked at her phone. "A guy named Tony is going to pick us up on Kay Lane in ten point two minutes. We can cut through that path to the park."

"You are not talking me into this. You can just forget it right now."

Fifteen minutes later, we were in an Uber with a guy named Tony, Pam's wheelchair tucked away in the trunk, driving towards Atlanta. I knew I had crossed a line into madness.

CR•SO

Dear Crabigail,

My husband has an ugly green recliner, and I would like to replace it with a loveseat. I'm afraid he'll get mad. Please advise.

Signed,
Wants to snuggle in Snellville

Dear Snuggy,

So, you see yerself snuggled up with yer man on this loveseat, rustling around like two cockroaches in a bowl of sugar? That ain't realistic atall. There's a reason God created recliners. Here's what's really gonna happen. You go right on ahead and haul off his recliner and get you a fancy loveseat with big ole frilly flowered pillows. He's gonna come in from mowing the lawn, strip off his sweaty shirt and plop down on yer loveseat shedding back hairs, sweat, and chiggers all over it. When he realizes he can't stretch hisself out enough, then he's gonna pile up all yer throw pillows on the floor so he can lay across em and balance his beer on top of his belly. Then yore dog rushes over for a petting, knocking the beer into the pile of Cheeto crumbs he's left in the floor. And where are you gonna sit? I'll tell ya where. You'll be sitting in a jail cell next to Maude, who's also facing murder charges, cause she thought buying a vibrating Jacuzzi would put some spark in her marriage.

Yers,
Crabigail

ભ•ଓ

CHAPTER 40
CONFESSION

Ryan stood in the back of the small hospital office. He and Jim learned on the way there that the DNA was, in fact, a match to the comatose doctor. It didn't take long to determine who they needed to interview.

Vivien, the nurse, was in tears as Agent Candor questioned her for the third time, this time on camera.

"I didn't know anyone would get hurt. I swear it."

"How did this woman, Diana, approach you the first time?"

"She came here often. She said Mr. . . . Dr. Armstrong was her father."

"Go on."

"We talked a lot. Mostly in the dining room. I could tell she cared about him."

"Anything strange about her behavior?"

"No. She seemed normal." There was a pause. "Except sometimes, she would do this weird tapping thing on her head and chest." Vivien demonstrated.

"What was it for? Do you know?"

"No idea. It was strange. Over time, I got used to it. She's been coming here for about a year."

"How did the sperm retrieval come up?"

Vivien looked down at her lap, embarrassed. "It wasn't one conversation. It was lots of them. Diana'd talk about how no one was left in her family to carry on the genes. She said her father had a brilliant mind and wasn't it a shame to not pass it on. I guess she hadn't got to go to college, or anything like that, like her dad had. She was very smart. It was a waste, you know."

"Did she talk about her mother?"

"I asked her about her mom a couple of times. She'd just clam up, and her eyes would get spooky. I've never seen anything like it. Kind of scary. Black eyes. Black as night."

"Getting back to the sperm."

Vivien sighed and closed her eyes. "At some point, she asked me to do it. She was going to use a surrogate to a . . . you know, carry on his genes. That's what she told me. He's such a good-looking man, and I know he liked it. He can't move or talk or anything, but some of his body parts work just fine."

"Did she pay you?"

"No. Not for that. I don't know why I agreed. It was wrong. I know it was wrong." Vivien burst into tears again.

"About the drugs. The succinylcholine? We know a vial is missing from the med room here."

"I'm going to jail. I know it. I gave it to her. She said it was for a pet."

"That's just not true, and you know it isn't true." Agent Candor slammed his hand on the desk making Vivien and Ryan both flinch.

"Okay, I sold it to her. I needed the money. Diana . . . she gave me five hundred dollars. I didn't ask what it was for. You don't know what it was like. I'd already done the other thing and . . . well it's her eyes; something scary there, that one. I . . . I just couldn't not do it. By then, I was scared to death to say no to her."

"How would she know how to administer it? Does she have medical training?"

"I don't know, sir. I guess she Googled it. You can find out anything nowadays."

Ryan had no sympathy for the woman. She was disgusting. The hospital would terminate her, she would serve some time, and he was glad for it.

"Do you know how to contact her?"

"No sir. She used to come here every Wednesday, but she hasn't come here since I gave her the . . . washcloth. I'm so sorry."

Both men felt the vibrations of their phones. Jim nodded to Ryan, and the young officer stepped into the hallway to take the call.

"Stand up, Vivien. Hands behind your back."

Jim motioned to the waiting female police officer. The officer placed handcuffs on Vivien's hands and began reading her the Miranda Rights. "You have the right to remain silent. You have the right to an attorney. If you do not have a . . . "

The door flew open. "Jim! Agent Candor, sir. We have to go. The Gardin twins are missing."

Agent Candor winced, grabbed his papers, and stuffed them quickly into his briefcase. As they exited Vivien said, "Sir I almost forgot. She's got a sister; a twin sister. I never met her. She didn't visit, but Diana talked about her a lot."

CR•SO

Dear Crabigail,

My boyfriend asked me to marry him, but all he gave me was a ring with a diamond so tiny I needed a magnifying glass to find it. Should I marry him?

Thanks,
Diamonds Are A Girl's Best Friend

Dear Diamond Digger,

I guess you've been hoodwinked like most women. Centuries ago, men started tricking us into thinking rocks were what we were hankering for, and most of y'all were dumb enough to fall for it. My late husband (he ain't dead, just late for dinner) tried to give me a cubic zirconia ring for my birthday. I threw it back at him, and told him if he wanted to make me happy, he should shave his head, put on a white t-shirt and pretend to be Mr Clean for two hours. He washed and waxed for about ten minutes before collapsing in his recliner, and slept till morning. Cause he didn't bother me none, I got control of the remote and watched "Dirty Dancing" twice. Best birthday ever! But, if you just gotta have a big rock, grab a fish net and head over to my house, cause I'm about to pass a kidney stone the size of a cantaloupe.

Yers,
Crabigail

છ•ઠ

CHAPTER 41
UBER GREAT TIME

Tony, the chubby, rosy-cheeked, quiet young man who drove us to Atlanta pulled into the parking deck at the Peachtree Rehabilitation Hospital. I figured he would go on his merry way, and we'd have to find another way home. I was wrong.

Pam tipped Tony a twenty, and asked him if he could eat lunch across the street at the diner. She told him that if he would, she'd pay for his lunch when we finished our visit, and then he could get a second fare taking us back. He was delighted of course, and happily helped Pam into her wheelchair. If I was Tony, I'd order every single thing on the menu.

I pushed Pam through the parking deck to the third level looking for the crossing bridge that would span across Peachtree Street and open to the wing where the Dr. resided. In hindsight, we should have had Tony drop us off at the front doors across and below. But, Mapquest had told me this was the shortest route to the floor we were going to visit. The crossing bridge was hard to find, and there weren't any direction signs that I could see. I was getting frustrated, when a blue car pulled in and began circling the lanes near us. The car pulled into a space a few feet away.

I pushed Pam's wheelchair slowly towards the car. A blonde woman exited. Maybe she could help. As we approached her, I froze. Pam put a warning hand over her shoulder onto my hand. We didn't speak. The woman was the spitting image of her father . . . The man from the phenotype. We knew it was his daughter, and she knew we knew it.

I tried to back up, but she came forward and pulled a gun from her pocket. Strange thing to notice, but I saw two Band-Aids on her wrist. "Over there." Diana gestured to an empty area concealed behind concrete pillars.

"Who are you?" I asked, not moving.

"Now!"

Pam was more mad than scared. "How did you find us?"

"Find you? I didn't know to look for you. You girls weren't even a blip on my radar at all. Twins just appear right in front of me in a deserted parking garage. I can't wait to tell my sister. She didn't send me to you like the others. She'll be surprised I found you on my own, without her help. Must be Karma."

Karma. Lord!

I pushed Pam's wheelchair to the area the woman was pointing to. There were ladders, boxes, boards, and a power saw plugged in there where someone appeared to have been working on a beam. The workers must have gone to lunch. A rope was tied to a beam up above and anchored to a ring set in the concrete floor. I spotted an Exacto knife laying on a cardboard box. I was trying to figure out a way to get to the Exacto when the woman tossed me a real knife. It clattered to the floor in front of me. It was huge with a leather handle, like hunters use.

"Pick it up," Diana said.

I did, very slowly. "Now what?"

"I want you to slice your sister's throat."

"I'm not going to do that,"

"Yes, you will. If you don't I'll start shooting her in the knees. Cut her, and it will be over fast."

"I'm not hurting my sister." With a MacGyver like motion, I swung the knife at the rope attached to the beam over the murderer's head.

Turns out, I'm not like MacGyver at all. I'm not even Mr. Magoo. I guess I'm more of a Wylie Coyote. The knife didn't cut so much as a hair of the rope. The impact of the attempt knocked it right out of my hand. The knife skittered across the concrete.

Diana laughed. "Wait til I tell my sister what you just tried to do." She laughed again.

Pam said, "Your sister is dead. Your mother killed her."

Diana's eyes darkened. It was like looking into the soul of a snake. Terrifying, those eyes. She lowered the gun, so that it was even with Pam's face.

"I know my sister is dead. Her soul still lives, though. I've been trying to help her rest. Don't you understand that?"

Pam was going to have answers no matter what. "How can you, as a twin, hurt other twins? Kill them?"

"You have your sister, and I'll have mine. I have most of the parts now to bury in my garden. Nobody ever cared to bury her, so she's still with me, haunting me. She calls me. I try to make her laugh when she calls. I can't help the things she makes me do, but sometimes I can make her wait awhile."

"You're crazy," I said.

Still looking at Pam and ignoring me she said, "I tell her jokes. She doesn't always get them, though. Do you know why the baby strawberry cried?"

She didn't seem to expect an answer from us. "Because his Mommy was in a jam." She laughed. "Get it? In a jam?"

Pam made a slight forward motion with her feet. Diana didn't seem to notice it, but I did.

I had no idea what to say, but I tried. "Have you seen the suffering on the face of the mothers? You killed their children. Why?"

Her eyes became blacker, then. I might not have chosen the best topic. Pam made the small kicking motion again. We don't always need to talk to communicate.

"I think I need your mouth." She looked up at me. "And yours. I need yours, too. Maybe just a piece of a lip. Pick that knife back up. I have to hurry. I have to see my father, today and Paul is coming home soon. I have a beef stew in the slow cooker. Still lots to do before he gets home."

"I'm not picking it up. There are police all over the place here." I didn't know if that was true at all. "If you shoot that gun, they'll hear it. They'll come running. Don't try it."

Diana pulled the hammer on the gun Paul had bought her the year before. He liked to take her to shooting practice before they went on a deer hunt. Paul always took Diana hunting with him, not so much for the company, but for her skills at skinning and cutting up the kill. Paul would brag to his friends that Diana could cut up a deer like a surgeon.

"Pick it up, NOW!

Diana stepped closer. The pupils in her eyes were as black as a frying pan.

I should have been terrified, but I wasn't. My hands were on Pam's wheelchair. This awful woman wanted me to hurt my sister. What I felt was outrage. I could feel my anger reach Pam. I looked down and saw her grip the sides of her chair. She kicked a third time . . . a signal. I didn't think about what I was going to do. I just did it. I pushed Pam's chair as hard as I could. Pam stuck her feet out, striking the woman hard in the stomach. The gun fired. The impact of feet to gut knocked the woman back and the gun up. The bullet ricocheted around the garage, and I was afraid it would find a home in one of our skulls.

Coughing, Diana staggered to her feet and aimed the gun at me, again. I closed my eyes as I heard the explosion, then a thump.

I screamed. "PAM!"

I opened my eyes. The woman lay on the ground. Her eyes were open, but the evil blackness had turned opaque. Blood pooled from the woman's chest. I looked beyond the concrete pillar and saw Ryan. White faced and trembling, Ryan had shot her dead.

When the young officer left the hospital on his mission to find us, he had walked briskly towards the waiting patrol car at the curb near the hospital's front doors. Jim was close behind him. With the first gun shot, both men broke into a run across the hospital grounds, darted around screeching, braking vehicles on busy Peachtree Street, to the vast public parking garage. The younger, former quarterback reached the third level first.

Agent Candor arrived within seconds. He calmly took the gun from Ryan's shaking hands, still in the air . . . both hands on the grip . . . the way he was trained.

Pam looked up at me from her wheelchair. "Told you the trip would be worth it."

Lord.

CR•ED

CHAPTER 42
AFTER SHOCK

Ryan was at the bar with his dad, sipping a beer. His dad noted how much taller his son appeared even sitting on a bar stool. His normal slump was gone.

"And then what happened, Son?"

"I guess that was it. I had to hand over my badge and gun while the GBI investigates. I'm on administrative duty until that's done."

"I don't think that's such a bad thing. You could use a rest."

"I'm fine. It's all routine."

"How about you? You sleeping okay, Son? You having nightmares? You used to get them a lot when you were a youngun. All them scary movies you watched."

"I'm fine Dad. I'll see a shrink this week. Part of what they're making me do. I had no choice but to shoot that woman."

"That's right. You saved two lives, probably more. Why was she cutting up the bodies? Do you know?"

"It's crazy. I think she suffered the same mental illness as her mother. Like her mother, she could pass easily for sane to most people if they didn't look too long at her eyes. I saw her eyes, Dad." Ryan shivered. "They were evil. Anyway, her mother killed the twin sister when she killed herself. Diana survived, and was raised by an aunt, her mother's sister. Apparently, the aunt felt it was necessary to let her ward know every gruesome detail, including where her father was, and what her mother had done. Diana wanted to bury the sister that haunted her, and she wanted to punish her own mother by punishing her victim's mothers. How sick is that? She was very intelligent like her parents, but uneducated. The doctors we've interviewed say it's all a dangerous combination. That's the theory anyway."

"I've always said, History don't repeat itself, but it shore does rhyme."

Ryan smiled. He'd heard his dad say that many times.

"Your mother wants to see you. Dinner tomorrow night?"

"Sure, Dad."

"Bring Candy. Your mom wants to meet her."

"We'll be there. Thanks, Dad."

Ryan's phone rang. It was Jim.

"You still with your dad, Ryan?"

"Yes, Sir. I am."

"I just wanted to check in on you. You did an incredible job, Ryan. You should be proud. Get a little more experience under your belt, and then give me a call. We might have a place for you here at Quantico.

Ryan was surprised. "Thanks Jim. That's certainly something to think about. You still in town?"

"I am. Paperwork, you know. Your dad called me earlier, and invited me to dinner tomorrow. Told me to bring a date."

Ryan looked at his dad and laughed. "He did, huh? You got one, Jim?"

"Maybe. I've got a real pretty redhead I'm thinking of calling."

CR•SO

Dear Crabigail,

Do you have a good recipe for brownies? Mine are dry and taste just awful.

Signed,
Fortunate to Have an Understanding Boyfriend

Dear Misfortune,

Pick yerself up a box of Little Debbie's Brownies over at the Hoggly Woggly and stick em in a pan. Long as yer the one that takes off the cellophane wrappers, means you can claim you made em.

Yers,
Crabigail

☙•❧

EPILOGUE
MOM'S STORY

A few days after my last interview with the press and the police, I drove Pam back home to Rome. Pam glowed from all the attention, and I let her enjoy it. I would yell at her later for, once again, nearly getting us killed.

I arrived back in Carrollton around noon, and was delighted to see a For Sale Sign at the edge of our yard. Dan had called a realtor that morning to put our house on the market. We were really going to retire to Myrtle Beach. My husband was in the house enjoying a peanut butter and jam sandwich. I was glad that he'd found his jam, and hadn't noticed one was still missing. The girls and I had, in fact, consumed a jar of his blackberry jam while he was at the Masters in April. I smiled as I parked, and then walked back up the driveway to check the mail.

I opened my mailbox and pulled out a thick white envelope with extra postage glued crookedly in the right corner. The return address showed that it was from my mother. I smiled, again. "She did it." I would make a strong cup of coffee in the Keurig, settle in my rocker, and then savor every word she'd written.

As I carried the envelope up the driveway, my phone rang from the recesses of my pocket. It was Lizzie.

"EEEEEK! I have a dinner date tonight."

"Who? Who are you going out with?"

"You will never believe it in a million years. Guess!"

"Ummm. Andy Davis."

"Nope."

"The guy from Match that liked gerbils?"

Lizzie had no intention of letting me continue to guess. "Nope. That very handsome, gorgeous FBI guy, Agent Candor. Do you think it's creepy that his name is Jim? Can I marry two Jims?"

"You're kidding! And no, it's not creepy. A widow jumping into marriage before the first date might be, though. I'm really happy for you. Pam will be devastated. You have a date with Shemar. I can't wait to tell her."

Lizzie laughed. It was good to chat about normal things, again.

"Hey, Lizzie."

"What?"

"I don't think there are any rattlesnakes in Washington D.C. Not the reptile kind anyway."

"Ha! Very funny."

"You go and have a wonderful time. I approve. I really do."

"What should I wear? Something colorful. No. He's a Fed. Probably black with pearls. Something understated but elegant. Come over and help me choose."

"Okay. I will. Gotta read a letter from Mom first, then I'm on the way."

"Jim said something really odd to me on the phone. We've been talking for a couple weeks, by the way. He called me a few times while y'all were up in D.C. to keep me up to speed he said, but I could tell he was interested. I didn't want to jinx it by telling you."

"What was the odd thing? What did he say?"

"He asked me if I could handle a Gee You relationship. Do you know what that is?"

"I have no idea. I expect you will ask him. I'll see you in half an hour."

I settled into my chair with coffee and letter. Dan was outside trimming hedges, my cat was sleeping, and Judy . . . well, they're always quiet. My house was peaceful. I couldn't wait any longer.

. . . .

Late one fall afternoon, I was walking out to my grandmother's house. I had walked the narrow dirt road to her house many times, since I was a very young child. She was my Daddy's mama. I called her "Mamaw." I loved her dearly, and she delighted seeing me come to spend the night, especially after Pappaw left her. My Mamaw talked non-stop at times, and often about people and things I knew nothing about. She suffered from mental illness, and sometimes, I could hear her outside talking to herself. For religious reasons, never explained, she only washed her hair once a year, and would have me sit at night and scratch her scalp. I did this dutifully for her for years.

Mamaw had been in a mental hospital during extreme periods of paranoia, and would sadly, eventually die there. I loved my Pappaw, but unable to deal with Mamaw's increasing mental episodes, he had moved in with one of their daughters about fifty miles away.

One day after Pappaw had left, I spent the night with Mamaw, and my cousin Edith had come over to keep me company. Mamaw kept us up all night digging through the drawers in our room looking for "Mottos." We had no idea what she was talking about.

As he did every morning, Daddy came out the next morning to stoke her fire. He managed to calm her down. Mamaw finally settled into her chair to listen to J Harold Smith, a con artist radio preacher that she often sent her meager money to.

Edith and I escaped outside, and began sweeping the porch and yard. In those days, no one had a lawn, so you had to keep the packed dirt free of debris with a broom. Suddenly, the screen door slammed open and Mamaw yelled, "STOP! You'll step over God's Three Deadlines!"

Dealing with Mamaw's craziness was better than living at home where my brothers liked to torture me by tearing pages out of my beloved comic books, and dinners were a melee of forking food across the table. If I was there, I took my plate to the room I shared with two sisters, while my brothers taunted me with, "There goes Queen Bee." It's amazing how much I grew up to love those boys.

More often than not, probably five days out of seven, I walked the long dirt road to Mamaw's. I had such wonderful memories of my beloved Pappaw, and I missed him now that he had moved away. Unlike my chatty Mamaw, he was a very quiet man. Everyone called him "Toby." He delighted in telling me stories and playing games with me.

One day, when I was a little girl, maybe three or four, Pappaw told me that, if I ran around the house three times, there would be two little calves following me. My father and grandfather were both farmers and raised a good bit of cattle, so I was very excited. I ran around the house as he had instructed, and that is when I learned, through his laughing explanation, that the soft back parts of my little legs from the knees down were called "calves."

Another time, Pappaw took me to the little town of Calhoun, riding in his old buck-board wagon pulled by two mules. This is the same town we moved you kids to when your dad was in Vietnam. Anyway, it was a hot summer day, and Pappaw had stopped to break off a leafy tree branch for me to shade my head. It was an all-day trip there and back to buy a few supplies. It wasn't really adventurous, but I cherish that memory . . . riding silently and closely beside my Pappaw.

Sadly, after he left, I only got to see my grandfather once or twice a year. Our families were dirt poor. My Daddy would work the fields from sun-up to sun-down, raising crops to sell and to feed his family. He also raised tobacco to sell in the winter, cut pulpwood to sell at the paper mill in Calhoun, and set traps in the nearby branch where he caught muskrats and an occasional mink.

I had watched my Daddy skin one of those creatures when I was a young girl, and I was horrified. Daddy had these boards that he made that he stretched the skin inside out and over. He would then use his pocket knife to scrape the bloody flesh off. Daddy would have rails of skins hanging to dry. One day, I watched him wipe that knife off across his overalls leg, then cut an apple in half. He offered me half of it. He laughed and laughed at my reaction and refusal. After that, I made sure I wasn't around when Daddy brought something home from the traps.

I loved my Daddy and knew he did his best to make sure us eight kids were fed every day. But there were lots of things my family ate that I could not. I never ate poke salad, souse meat, fat back . . . not a single speck . . . squirrel meat, and most definitely an apple cut by a nasty knife. Because of this, instead of "Betty," my brothers and sisters called me, "Queen Bee." I didn't care, and would just leave them all, and walk up the dirt road to stay the night with Mamaw.

Thinking about my chances of making the basketball team, I began the walk to Mamaw's that fall day. I had just turned fifteen and had entered high school. I was five foot ten with long legs, and I could make good time if I wanted, but I liked to stroll leisurely and enjoy the sights. I slowed to admire the red clay bank on the right. Some of the tree roots were exposed, leaving deep indentations that looked like tiny caves or places frogs could find refuge on a rainy day. The narrow road wound through the forest, meadows and some of the fields where my daddy, and his daddy before him, grew crops. I spotted Daddy walking down to the barn to feed the hogs, mules, horses and cows and waved at him.

The road to Mamaw's was about a mile long. I would always carry with me books to read. I loved comic books, especially horror ones about ghosts, vampires, and other weird creatures. My very favorite were werewolves . . . the scarier the story, the better. I also had a copy of Grimm's

Fairy Tales. Nancy Drew had replaced The Bobbsey Twins as I entered high school, and I took those, too.

I dreamed one day that I would meet my prince, and live happily ever after. Sometimes, I would carry moss to the place under those exposed tree roots, and imagine little people coming out at night to dance in the moonlight. I had a vivid imagination. I may have grown up poor, but I had treasures that I bet city kids never had, and this road was one of them.

I turned to a bend in the road where a large tree had summer grapes growing on vines high up in its top. The grapes were way too high to reach. My younger sister, Linda, and I had walked out there many a late evening, and had tried throwing sticks in the air to knock the fruit down. We rarely ever succeeded, but when we did!!! Oh my!!!

The tree was not one we could climb, and we usually had to be content with the low hanging vines that we could hook with a stick, and pull down close enough to pluck. The tree was loaded that year. The grapes would be ripe enough to eat in a couple more weeks, and I couldn't wait. Wild grapes are smaller than the ones people grow in vineyards, and very tart, but Linda and I loved them.

I left the grapes and continued to a curve in the dirt road. I froze in my tracks. A large furry, brown animal was standing on its hind legs, munching on weeds. It was pulling the weeds up, and holding them with its smaller front paws. Its back feet were huge.

Growing up in the country as I had, I thought I knew every kind of animal native to the area. I knew immediately what it was not, but had no idea what it was! I laid down my Nancy Drew books and comics as quietly as I could. I began to walk slowly toward the creature.

My intention was to see how close I could get to it before it ran away. The wind must have been blowing away from me, because the animal didn't seem to smell me. I moved closer and closer, tiny steps at a time until I was a foot away. Still, it stood there munching away. Without thinking, I lunged and grabbed the back of its neck with my right hand. At the same time, I used my left hand to take hold of his big hind legs.

The creature was squealing and struggling like crazy to free itself, but I held on. I held it away from my body as I could see its sharp claws. Completely horrified at what I had done, but not knowing how to safely let it go, I began running back toward my home, screaming for my Daddy.

I held on tight, terrified to let go for fear that it would attack me before it was out of my outstretched hands. I just kept running as hard as I could yelling, "Help me Daddy, Help me!" My long legs were my friends that day. Near the barn, I saw my Daddy throw his bucket down. He ran toward me as hard as he could to see what was wrong.

When Daddy saw what I was holding, he hollered something like, "Good God Almighty! That thing could eat you up!" I was crying and saying, "Get it Daddy. Get it!" Daddy told me to hold it as tight as I could til he could get his hands in position to replace mine. Once he did, he told me to let go suddenly and run out of the way. I did just that. Once my Daddy had it under control, with a sudden quick motion, he slammed its head on the nearby chopping block that he used to cut firewood. It killed the animal instantly. The meat and the fur would be harvested for the family.

My daddy gave me a good scolding. He told me that the animal was a large female groundhog. He made me swear I'd never do such a fool thing again, and I promised I wouldn't. And, I didn't . . . til a few months later, when I snuck up on and caught a huge Big Brown Bat . . . that's their actual name . . . by the wings and ran home to Daddy, screaming for help.

. . . .

My thoughts went to Diana. How could anyone want to punish my Mom? That's who would suffer most if we had been killed. My Mom!

My mother has led such a full and rewarding life. She's raised wonderful children, even including Brett. Despite a hard upbringing, she loved and was loved. She cherished her parents and siblings. She adored my dad, and she fiercely loved us.

Mom served those in her community, first as the wife of a Veteran, and then as a caring, talented nurse. She was a dedicated volunteer for Cherry Log Christian Church, Feed Fannin and the Clothes Closet, all organizations that help families in need. She will one day, a long time from now, leave quite a legacy.

I absolutely loved her story. With a little encouragement I bet we could get her to write some more. I called her to tell her my thoughts, and to thank her.

Mom said, "You're welcome. I'm in the middle of making those Three Wiseman Sausage balls. I used hot sausage, not sage. Let me wipe my hands."

I waited.

She returned, shortly. "You do understand the purposefulness of the story don't you?"

"Purposefulness?" I had no idea what she meant.

"The moral of the story?" she asked impatiently.

"Ummmm . . . Don't be catching critters like groundhogs and bats with your bare hands?"

"NO!" She sighed louder than Dan ever did. "It means that sometimes people have fears that are just crazy like my grandmother. Then, there are fears that are legitimate, like catching wild animals with your hands. It means that when there is a serial killer targeting twins, and when you're caring, loving Mother warns you about it, you better well take it seriously."

"Lord! Love You Mom."

CR•ʔᴏ

Dear Crabigail,

I want to buy my wife the perfect Christmas gift. She loves books, and I found a first edition copy of Pride and Prejudice at a used book store. Even though it's in mint condition, I'm wondering if that's enough, or should I get something else?

Yours,
Bookstore Bobby

Dear Bookstore Booby,

You must be smoking the wrong end of yer pipe iffin you think your poor wife wants some raggedy book that stinks so bad they had to stick mints on it. Why on earth would you get her a used book anyways, when there's some great new ones out there? I bet a cheap guy like you borrowed my book from yer neighbor's sister's cousin and now it's all dog-eared with notes writ in the margins. So get yerself on Amazon and buy her a brand new copy of "Dear Crabigail." In fact, buy one for yer Mama, yer Sister, and even yer Daddy (iffin he can read). I hear tell ya can buy em in bulk.

Yers,
Crabigail

ભ•ા

www.dearcrabigail.com

A Berry College graduate, Penny Gardin Lewis began her career as an Industrial Arts teacher. Heavily involved with the Carroll County Community Theatre, she first served as a volunteer building sets, and later became the CPRCAD's Arts Coordinator and then its Arts Manager. She was the inaugural director of the Carrollton Cultural Arts Center, where she built Carrollton's reputation as a leader in the visual, literary and performing arts in Georgia. Her unique talent for engaging audiences led to many memorable performances and gallery shows highlighting local actors, musicians, dancers, writers and artists. In 2002, she launched MeccaFest, a juried arts festival, to celebrate national artists and showcase Carrollton's vibrant art community.

With the help of her husband, Dan and other collaborators, she has written and produced 38 musicals for children in the past 27 years, which have been performed by children all over the world.

Penny is enjoying semi-retirement in Myrtle Beach, South Carolina writing novels, creating art, and hanging at the beach where happiness comes in waves. Her first two novels, Bearing Crosses and Microwave is Dead, were published in 2017 and earned Penny two Georgia Author of the Year nominations. (Bearing Crosses for Best First Novel and Microwave is Dead for Best Literary Fiction.)

Penny and Dan are parents to grown and gone children Meagan (Jeff), Leslie (David),and Chris (Sarah). They are eagerly waiting the birth of their first little grand child. Penny's next book will most likely be for that baby girl.

www.ingramcontent.com/pod-product-compliance
Lightning Source LLC
Chambersburg PA
CBHW070927250626
47159CB00009B/3145